A Candlelight Ecstasy Romance™

CANDLELIGHT ECSTASY ROMANCES™

LEAVES OF FIRE, FLAME OF LOVE

Susan Chatfield

A CANDLELIGHT ECSTASY ROMANCE™

Published by
Dell Publishing Co., Inc.
1 Dag Hammarskjold Plaza
New York, New York 10017

Dell ® TM 681510, Dell Publishing Co., Inc.

Candlelight Ecstasy Romance ™ is a trademark of
Dell Publishing Co., Inc., New York, New York.

ISBN: 0-440-14937-1

Printed in the United States of America

First printing—February 1981
Second printing—November 1981

Dear Reader:

In response to your enthusiasm for Candlelight Ecstasy Romances™, we are now increasing the number of titles per month from two to three.

We are pleased to offer you sensuous novels set in America, depicting modern American women and men as they confront the provocative problems of a modern relationship.

Throughout the history of the Candlelight line, Dell has tried to maintain a high standard of excellence, to give you the finest in reading pleasure. It is now and will remain our most ardent ambition.

Vivian Stephens
Editor
Candlelight Romances

Dedicated to A.H.F.:
For the idea of a story set in a
New England autumn and for your encouragement,
criticism and love.
S.C.

LEAVES OF FIRE, FLAME OF LOVE

Chapter One

The tinkle of ice cubes in the tall, cold glass drew Lindsay's attention away from her quiet contemplation of the sun sparkling upon the water of the swimming pool. Her attention turned to the friends she had invited over to enjoy the pool. Their shrieks and laughter pierced the stillness of the Washington, D.C. afternoon and, with a slight sense of distaste, Lindsay wondered why she had allowed these loud people to intrude upon the peaceful silence that she suddenly felt she needed so desperately.

She closed her eyes and sat back in the recliner, her lips tight. What was the matter with her? Normally she would have looked forward to an afternoon of fun with her pleasure-loving friends. Shaking her head slightly, Lindsay felt the sudden pressure of someone sitting down at the end of the chair.

Turquoise eyes flew open and took in the grinning face of her dearest friend, Debbie. Debbie's candid brown eyes noted the troubled look on Lindsay Sheffield's face. A tiny hand reached out and patted Lindsay's fingers, a gesture that normally would have bothered her. She hated to be fussed over.

"What's the matter, Lindsay? You've not been yourself all day."

With a deep sigh, Lindsay gazed at the concerned look

on her friend's small face. Of all the young people her age that she knew in Washington, only Debbie could be called a friend. The others fell into the category of acquaintances only.

Shaking her head slightly, Lindsay allowed a slight smile to form on her full lips. Her long, shoulder-length hair shone with blue-black lights. Shrugging slim shoulders, she said lightly, "Nothing's wrong, Debbie. Your imagination's working overtime, my friend."

Debbie shook her head. "You're not kidding me, Lindsay. Something is wrong . . . has been wrong for a long time. You're not yourself lately. What is it, Lindsay?"

Lindsay looked down into her glass, staring at the melting ice cubes as if they might give her the answer. Yes, there was something wrong, but she didn't know what. She didn't understand. She looked up at Debbie and whispered in a husky voice, "I'm sorry, Debbie, you're right. I don't know what's bothering me. I feel so restless—almost bored with my life. I can't explain the feeling. Here I am, twenty years old and an adult, and yet I feel at times that I've lived two hundred and twenty years. It's almost as if life is passing me by and I haven't accomplished anything, nothing that I'm proud of. Oh, I told you, it's silly—I can't explain it!" She grimaced in frustration and took a sip of her cold drink, shaking her head.

Debbie's brown eyes widened and she shook a disapproving finger at her friend. "You're bored? I don't believe it! How can you say that, Lindsay Sheffield! Why, any girl would give her right arm to be in your position! Why, look at you. You're young and beautiful, and wealthy in your own right. You've got a father who worships the ground you walk on, and he's a powerful political figure—a senator! You've got a reputation as the best hostess in Washington, everyone hopes to be invited to one of your parties. To top it all off, you've managed to snag one of the most handsome and eligible bachelors around, leaving all the rest of us single girls sitting back twiddling our thumbs in envy. Why, just look at that rock that Alec gave you. It's beautiful! How can you say you're bored? Your name is constantly in the newspapers. Women copy your clothes and your latest hair style. You'll make a perfect wife for Alec with your political background and beauty."

"Yes, won't I?" murmured Lindsay. Her eyes fell on the ring that Alec had given her to seal their engagement two months earlier. She sighed. It was large, almost too large for her taste.

Lindsay stared up at the passing clouds as they drifted by in the clear blue of the late summer sky. Fall would soon be here, bringing gray, overcast days to the capital. People would then flock indoors, and Lindsay could almost predict the inevitable parties and get-togethers that would follow. She would assume the important role as hostess for her father and his future son-in-law, Alec Clarke.

Her lips formed a half-smile as she thought of Alec. He had been on her father's staff when they had moved permanently to Washington. Her father felt that Alec's services were invaluable, and had entrusted him with many important matters. Alec was ambitious, Lindsay had always known that, and she had no doubt that he would move ahead in the political arena quite rapidly. Her father had been very pleased when their casual dates had culminated in an engagement.

As usual, the press had made much of their courtship, and Lindsay had ironically made note that perhaps it was the constant attention paid to them by the press that had caught Alec's eye, and not the girl he was with. Alec had not thought the remark funny. He was serious, handsome with his blond hair and cool blue eyes, and she knew he would make the perfect husband. Indeed, she thought, they would make the prefect couple, her dark good looks contrasting with his sophisticated fairer ones.

Then why was she so discontent? What was gnawing at her? Her future was secure. She could almost predict how many children they would have and the type of house they would live in. Perhaps when they were married she would no longer be hounded by the press. It seemed that she couldn't even go for a walk these days without being accosted by the damn newspaper reporters, always intruding into her privacy. Her feelings with regard to the press and the local gossip mongers who wrote the scandal sheets for them was notorious. She was Senator Raymond Sheffield's daughter, and therefore fair game. She was certain most of the country—and in particular, Washington—believed what was printed about her. Even though she knew that most of it was untrue, she couldn't deny the fact that she ran with a crowd that loved noise and fun. Lindsay had always maintained a cool exterior when confronted with one of the many escapades that she had been a part of stared back at her from the front of a daily newspaper, but she knew deep down that she would never bring shame to her father's good name.

She would declare hotly that the press had distorted the facts and would announce loftily that she was going to sue the next paper that printed an unflattering picture of her. Then she would go out with her friends, and her father would smile and shake his head. He knew his daughter too well. She was her mother all over again, quick to anger and just as quick to forgive. She was popular with the people surrounding her, and therefore must pay the price of being in the public eye. There was no room for privacy in politics, he had gently warned her.

She frowned. Her father had understood her attitude toward her privacy, and yet Alec seemed to encourage the press. He always made a point of making a generous comment to one of the local columnists if one spied them while they were out to dinner.

Annoyed with herself for being in this restive mood, Lindsay sat upright, determined to push aside such unloyal thoughts. Alec was what she wanted, and she was just going through a period of pre-nuptial jitters. Her father approved the marriage and his approval should be sufficient. For as far back as she could remember, he had always wanted what was best for her, and she in return had only wanted to please him and make him happy because she loved him.

14

He had been both father and mother to her. Her mother had died when she was twelve, just when her father had been in the middle of a budding political career. His dedication to his child and to his career had helped him through the traumatic time. He had lost the only woman he had ever loved, a lovely Irish woman much too young and beautiful to die the tragic way she did in an unavoidable automobile accident. He had picked up the pieces of his life and carried on, setting an example for his daughter.

Lindsay smiled at Debbie. "Don't worry so, Deb. I'm not going to throw it all away, if that's what you're afraid of. You're absolutely right. I have everything a girl could want, so I have no reason to feel useless and bored. I'm just spoiled, that's all. Ignore me!"

She stood up and gathered her bathrobe from a stool. "I'm going in now. Alec is coming over tonight and hopefully we'll be able to spend some time together without Father's and his getting into another discussion on the latest bill to be drafted." Debbie laughed, nodded, and walked over to a group of friends who were sitting around the pool, preparing to leave.

After saying good-bye to everyone, Lindsay walked into the large Georgian house and on up the stairs to her bedroom. She gazed on the soft peach and cream walls and deeper-shaded peach shag carpet. The ivory satin comforter covering her large bed seemed to beckon and with a sigh she slowly walked over to it. Perhaps she was just tired and needed a small nap.

Long, slim fingers reached up to automatically rub the throbbing in her temple. Lindsay reached down and folded the comforter to the end of the soft, inviting bed. Slipping out of her robe, she quickly peeled off her bathing suit and walked into her bathroom.

Without taking time to enjoy the beauty of the hand-wrought mosaic tiling on the walls or to take in the cooling colors of blue and white intermingled with the fresh green of hanging plants, she turned on the shower and stepped in. She was in no mood for a bubble bath,

15

which she usually preferred, scented with bath salts and perfumes.

After her shower, Lindsay dried herself as she walked from the bathroom. The dark, quiet room calmed her and she slipped beneath the cool sheets and pulled the ivory blanket up over her shoulders.

A sound caused a sleep-filled Lindsay to stir. Was it voices from downstairs or had it been her imagination? Stirring from a cocoon of dark and easy sleep, Lindsay lifted her head from the downy softness of the feather pillows. Her black hair fell about her face and her turquoise eyes were cloudy with sleep. She looked like a child who had been awakened in the middle of the night.

She turned an ear toward the door. Yes, she had heard a voice, a deep, decisive voice filled with laughter. Perplexed, she pushed back the covers and stepped out of bed. Shivering, she realized that she had forgotten to put on a nightgown. Frowning, she quickly grabbed a bathrobe and slipped it on. Running across the soft carpet, she reached the door and opened it a crack.

She hadn't recognized the voice and wondered who it belonged to. She knew most of her father's friends and business acquaintances but none possessed the quality and strength of this man's voice. Straining to see who was talking to Emerson, the butler, she glimpsed only a pair of shoes, handsome dark business shoes made of an obviously expensive soft leather, and long legs dressed in a dark silk business suit. She could not see above the slim hips, and moved forward quietly and inconspicuously to try to get a glimpse of the man who stood in such a relaxed, yet proud stance.

A sudden creak at the top of the landing caused eyes, as black as coal and sparkling as black diamonds, to glance quickly up to where Lindsay stood. She caught only a glimpse of the tanned, angular face as she immediately stepped backward.

Feeling guilty at spying, she held her breath and grasped the front of her bathrobe together over slightly

16

heaving breasts. Had he seen her? No. The voices continued and she heard the click of the front door. Feeling ridiculous, Lindsay quickly ran to the front window and
looked down at the tall man who was leaving the house.
His walk was easy and graceful, yet somehow it exuded an
animallike strength. Black hair gleamed in the sun, thick,
straight and healthy. The man came to a stop in front of a
Mercedes sport coupe and hesitated for a brief moment,
his head to one side. It was as if he knew she was
watching him. Lindsay stepped back from the window
quickly, her heart thumping.

With a slight smile, the unidentified man's watchful
black eyes darted up to the window as he lowered his lean
and powerfully built body into the car. Lindsay gazed with
admiration as the driver then pulled the Mercedes out into
traffic and disappeared around a corner. She thought it ap-
propriate that the color of the car was gleaming black. A
brightly colored or flashy car would not have suited the
proud, dark stranger.

With a half-smile on her lips, Lindsay walked away
from the window and wandered back to her room to dress.
Whimsically, she wondered who the dark man might be.
How did her father come to know him? Shrugging her
shoulders, Lindsay dismissed the episode from her mind as
she concentrated on picking out a dress for that night.
Alec liked the more sophisticated styles, so she chose a
dark blue and silver dinner sheath with a halter neckline.
It would go well with her dark hair and the silver seemed
to make her azure eyes sparkle, an effect she needed at
this moment. Perhaps she needed a vacation. Yes, suddenly the idea of getting away from Washington appealed
to her.

Smiling, Lindsay looked at her reflection in the mirror.
Just the idea had already brought a splash of color to her
cheeks, highlighting her fragile cheekbones. She added a
dab of peach gloss to her full, sensual lips and a touch of
black mascara to her already thick, dark lashes. A touch
of blush to her cheeks and she was ready to meet Alec.
Lindsay reached for a small bottle of Fidji that her father

had given her and dabbed it behind her ears, over her long neck and upper arms. She smiled as she remembered what her father had told her when he had given it to her—it was just a small part of an island but the sweetest-smelling part.

An island! That's where she should go. Perhaps Bermuda! Of course. Why hadn't she thought of it sooner? She needed the relaxing ways of an island sun and the peaceful sounds of soft waves breaking on a quiet beach. A place where there would be no newshounds following her around, writing down everything she did and everything she said. She'd tell Alec and her father tonight!

Lindsay gathered a silk evening coat from her closet and walked happily from the room, stepping lightly down the staircase. As she laid the coat on the settee in the foyer, she turned to enter the living room. Emerson walked into the room with dignity, carrying a tray with coffee and tiny sandwiches, a slight smile on his face as he took in the beauty of this young girl who had emerged from the childhood tragedy of losing her mother to become a fine young woman.

"Here, Miss Lindsay, I thought you might feel the need of a slight repast as you didn't eat any lunch earlier." He laid the tray on a coffee table of polished teak.

Lindsay reached for a cup of strong, hot coffee and bit hungrily into a cucumber sandwich as she gazed up at Emerson innocently and asked, "Who was the dark man you were talking to earlier in the foyer? I woke up and heard voices." She finished the tiny sandwich and reached for another.

"Oh, that gentleman stopped for a moment to see your father. He didn't wish me to wake you, and as your father was still at his meeting and wouldn't return until later this evening, he just left a message that he had passed through. He was only passing Washington briefly, I assume, and was in a hurry to leave for his home. He said he would phone your father later on. I gathered they are old acquaintances, Miss Lindsay. A man of few words, he was. Still waters, if you understand me, miss?"

Lindsay smiled at hearing Emerson's evaluation of the dark stranger. Still waters run deep. Yes, that would have been her description also. An old friend of her father's, and yet, she didn't know him. Oh, well, she sighed to herself. She didn't know every one of her father's associates.

Just as she was about to ask the man's name, the doorbell rang. Emerson turned swiftly and walked out into the foyer. Lindsay heard him greeting Alec quietly. Emerson didn't like Alec Clarke. Lindsay knew it and so did Alec. Her father had chuckled when Alec had bristled one evening and complained that Emerson didn't know his place. Lindsay had calmed Alec down and told him not to get upset, that Emerson had been with the family a long time and managed to maintain a constant air of dignity balanced by a sufferance for her shenanigans. After that, Alec had maintained a cool silence in Emerson's presence.

Lindsay stood up and smiled as Alec walked quickly toward her, his arms outstretched. He took her into his arms and held her tightly.

When Emerson left the room, Alec pulled Lindsay more tightly to him as his mouth descended on hers. Lindsay allowed Alec his possessive embrace and returned his kiss with enthusiasm as her arms circled his neck. Suddenly she saw a pair of black eyes mocking her and, feeling guilty for such disloyal thoughts, returned Alec's now demanding kiss with more passion than she felt.

Alec's body tightened, and he forced her lips apart in response to the passion she had ignited in him. Lindsay forced herself to accept his kiss, but when his hand reached for her halter to untie it, she froze, suddenly afraid of what she had started. She wondered if she would always freeze up like this when Alec touched her. Perhaps there was something wrong with her. She had never allowed a man to touch her and had never allowed the usual petting sessions with any of her dates go beyond kissing and a casual caress. She had certainly never felt the flashing ecstasy and fires that her girlfriends had spoken of so casually. She pulled away from Alec with a bright smile on her face.

19

"I'm famished, darling! Where are we dining tonight?" she asked, a trifle breathlessly. If Alec was bothered by her coolness, he didn't mention it. Cool blue eyes appraised her, almost as if he were about to purchase an object that he desired.

He smiled and answered, "You and your appetite again. You always think of your stomach first, and your heart second! Heartless woman you are, wench! Very well. I'll stuff you so full that you won't be able to run from me. I'll gather you up in my arms and carry you away to my attic and make mad, passionate love to you! Let's go!" He laughed, a picture of handsome good looks with his white teeth and blond hair. The laugh did not quite reach his eyes, and Lindsay again found herself wondering what it would have been like if a dark, tall stranger with eyes like black diamonds had taken her in strong arms and carried her off. She had the distinct feeling that he wouldn't have laughed. Snarled perhaps, she thought, bemused, but he would not have laughed. The thought brought a smile to her lips and she looked up at Alec and placed her hand in his as they walked out of the room together.

Alec laid the evening coat lightly over her shoulders and placed his hand gently over her elbow as he escorted Lindsay through the front door. As he opened the door of his large, shiny, silver Mark IV, Lindsay couldn't help but wonder if the automobile didn't reflect a larger part of Alec's personality. It was a car that people noticed, they noticed the driver as well. There was something indulgent about the car and Lindsay felt uncomfortable in it, despite its cushiony elegance. She felt as if she were part of the upholstery and that Alec was showing her off. Lindsay shrugged slightly and stared out the window, frowning. Why did she feel so discontented? She had never found fault with Alec before, or with her life. Debbie was right. She was the envy of all her friends and should be grateful for the good things she had. She was so lost in thought that she did not hear Alec talking to her. Suddenly she was brought back to reality when she felt the car pull to a stop and realized that they had arrived at the restaurant.

Lindsay turned to Alec and smiled. She would not spoil this dinner tonight. As she stepped out of the car and started to walk toward the door to the famous restaurant, she was suddenly blinded by the flash of a camera.

Lindsay halted and felt a surge of anger as her eyes tried to focus. With tightened lips she stood her ground, despite Alec's gentle efforts to move her into the restaurant. She felt ready to confront this photographer who had once again interrupted a private evening with her fiancé. She saw his now familiar face grinning at her. With flashing eyes that left no doubt of her displeasure, Lindsay turned to Alec as he whispered desperately in her ear, "Please, Lindsay, don't make another scene. Just ignore him! He's only doing his job! Try to act with dignity for once, darling, please!" He gazed down at her, his cool eyes pleading.

Lindsay forced a tight smile to her lips, and nodded slightly. "If that's what you want, Alec, but I do wish for once you would see my side of it. I almost believe you like to see your picture in the paper!" Lindsay bit her lip, regretting her sharp words as soon as she had spoken them. She avoided Alec's quick glance and marched into the restaurant, determined not to make another scene, if only for Alec's sake.

As they were led to their table set in a softly lit corner of the quiet dining room, Lindsay felt calmer. The room exuded softly understated elegance. As she sipped a pre-dinner martini, she gazed at Alec and noticed how quiet he had become. She looked into his reproachful eyes.

"I'm sorry, Alec," she whispered huskily. "I don't know what got into me. I've been so bitchy lately and you don't deserve it. Say you'll forgive me, darling?" She reached out her hand and he raised it to his lips, brushing the fingers with a quick kiss.

He watched Lindsay and carefully chose his words. His cool eyes watched the expression in her own troubled eyes as if searching for an explanation of her unusual behavior.

"I realize how you feel about these things, darling, but you must remember that as the wife of a politician and the daughter of a well-known senator, you are going to be exposed to this sort of thing every minute you are out of the house. You must learn to adjust and accept these slight intrusions into your private life. I should have thought by now, Lindsay, that you would have grown accustomed to the limelight and, being a mature woman, would have learned to ignore it. Really, my dear, please be a little more circumspect in your dealings with the press. You are starting to gain the reputation of disliking the press, and I must remind you, darling, that that same press can be most decidedly helpful in the political arena. It has been known to break the career of many a man who would not cooperate with them. I must ask you again, Lindsay, for my sake, for our future's sake, please don't antagonize them."

Lindsay listened quietly, an outward picture of coolness and calm. Inside she was seething with frustration and hurt. At least Alec could have understood. He could have tried to. Instead, he was putting everything into neat little categories and logically explaining to her how she should react. She bit her bottom lip and forced herself to listen as he droned on. She had lost her appetite and yearned for the privacy of her own room at home. Her head was throbbing and she placed long fingertips to her temples. Quickly, she burst out, interrupting, "Alec, I'm going away on a vacation. I have to get away to do some thinking." There, she had said it.

Alec stopped talking and gazed at her, eyes wide.

"What are you talking about, Lindsay? Why on earth would you go away by yourself? Why, in a few months we'll both be leaving on our honeymoon! You have important duties to attend to for your father and for me. We need you to hostess luncheons and dinner parties for us. You know how your father depends on you. No, now is definitely not the time to go off on a whim. You can't mean it, darling!" He frowned in disbelief.

"You just don't understand, do you, Alec? It's just because of these parties and luncheons and constant social affairs that I need to get away. I want to be by myself, to get my head together. Please, can't you see that if I can get away now, I'll come back rested and relaxed? You want a radiant bride walking down that aisle, don't you?" She gave him a winsome look.

"Really, Lindsay, I can't say I understand your impulsiveness. I don't see why you should feel discontented in the first place. Your father has spoiled you dreadfully, but you are not going to wind me around your little finger when we're married. I can't stop you from going away, but I certainly hope that when you return you'll stop this outlandish behavior. How will it look to Washington if I'm seen at social events without you at my side? Doesn't speak for much confidence in me, my dear." He looked crestfallen, very much like a small boy who had had his favorite toy taken away from him. Lindsay looked at him and shook her head gravely. He had left the decision to take a vacation in her hands, and she felt neither the guilt nor the happiness that she should have felt about the decision. Instead, for some reason she felt sad and empty. She was bewildered at this new awareness in her feelings toward Alec. If he had really cared one way or another, he would have taken a firm stand and have endorsed the idea or firmly said no. She felt deep disappointment. He had skirted the issue and failed to commit himself.

Lindsay looked up and said softly, "I'd like to go home now, Alec. I'm very tired. Let's skip dinner." Her eyes shone with determination, and Alec closed his mouth. He had been about to protest.

He stood up abruptly, threw some bills on the table, and walked over to Lindsay's chair to help her from the table. Lindsay sighed. He was always so correct. She wondered if Alec ever let his emotions control his actions. She had decided that he was ruled by his head, not his heart. She had used to think that that was a virtue and attribute in a leader.

Her father was a prime example. He always thought things over before making a decision, and rarely changed his mind once that decision was made. But then, her father had never lost touch with the human factor. His decisions were always based on what was good for the people he represented. Perhaps, she thought, it was this awareness of his fellow man that had made Raymond Sheffield such a strong and well-liked man in Washington.

She had always thought that Alec was like her father. Her father felt that Alec would go far in politics. She thought he had much to offer—dedication, youth, idealism, a strong sense of purpose. She knew how handsome and appealing he could be. But now she was wondering. Was it all a facade? Was her own life a facade—all decoration and frivolity? Had she no identity of her own?

As she slipped out of the car and walked to the house, Alec placed his arm around her shoulder and turned her toward him. She glanced up into his eyes.

"You know, Lindsay, I do love you," he said. "I only suggest what is for your own best interest, darling. You do see that, don't you?"

She nodded and bent her dark head. "Yes, Alec, I know you only want what is best for me. But I'm not sure if even I know what that is right now. That's why I'm going away for a few weeks. I'll go to Bermuda and stay in one of those tiny cottages on the beach where no one will know me."

Alec smiled indulgently. "Yes, darling, go if you must, but don't forget that you're hostessing a special party for me in three weeks. It's important that you be there. Why, you'll be even more ravishing than usual with your newly acquired tan. I'll be the envy of every man there." He smiled smugly, as if picturing it.

Lindsay smiled back wanly and nodded. "Yes, Alec, I remember the party and how important it is to you. You've been reminding me of it for the last month!" She chuckled. "You really are incorrigible, Alex. You seduce me with honey-coated words, just as you do your constituents. It's no wonder no one ever says no to you! Talk about being spoiled!" Her sudden laughter filled the cool night. Lindsay suddenly felt light-hearted. Alec slid his arms more securely around her waist and pulled her toward him in tight possession. Instinct immediately caused Lindsay to tighten up.

"Seduce you with words, my beauty? Yes, perhaps, but what is a man to do when the only word you know is a very definite 'no'?" With that he swooped down and took possession of her lips, now quivering in protest. As he tried to part her soft lips with his own hard ones, Lindsay placed a restraining hand on his chest and pushed him gently away.

"Please. Alec. I'm not in the mood. Perhaps after I return from Bermuda . . ." She left the rest unspoken, not understanding her sudden reluctance to have Alec make love to her.

With a taut goodnight, Alec turned and walked back to his car. Lindsay watched him, his head held high, and wondered at her stupidity. Yet she restrained an urge to call out to him that she was sorry. Frowning, she entered the lighted house and walked toward her father's study.

Lindsay stood in the doorway of the study, silently observing the silver-haired man who sat at the desk concentrating on what he was writing. She smiled to herself, love gleaming in her eyes. Quietly she walked over, laid her coat on a chair, and dropped a quick kiss on the top of his shining white head. She hugged him tightly and sat down on the corner of the desk, a smile wreathing her fragile face.

"Hello, Dad. You were late getting home tonight. Did the meeting go well?" Her eyes shone into his.

Raymond Sheffield carefully placed the pen he had been writing with down on the desk and leaned back to survey his daughter. It was no secret that father and daughter loved each other deeply. He watched her appraisingly. Despite the smile on her face, there was a shadow in her eyes.

"Reasonably so. I'm just writing down some additional memos to bring up later. Were you out with Alec?" he asked casually.

Lindsay frowned and stood up. She started to pace back and forth. "Dad, what would you say if I told you I wanted to go away—away from Washington for a while? Would you disapprove?"

Her father frowned and with a sigh asked, "And what makes you think I would disapprove? You've been on edge lately. I've noticed it, but haven't said anything. Is it something you want to talk about, honey? Can I help with anything?"

Lindsay stopped pacing and threw her arms out. She turned to her father and asked, "I wish there was something we could discuss, Dad, but I don't know what's wrong myself. That's why I want to get away where it's quiet, away from people. I've got to get my head straightened out, and I can't seem to do that here. Do you understand?" Her dark eyes beseeched him.

Dark blue eyes stared warmly back at her, noting the slight look of desperation on her face. "Has this something to do with Alec, Lindsay?"

Lindsay started, and looked down at her hands, concentrating on her fingertips. Finally she looked up into her father's eyes and answered. "I'm not certain. It's my life here, the routine, the social events, the parties, the people. Alec is part of all that, but it goes deeper. I feel like I'm missing something, Dad, and I don't know what it is or how to find it. Does that make any sense to you? 'Cause it sure doesn't to me."

Her father nodded and said softly, "Yes, I do understand. Your mother used to say the same thing when you were just a wee one. I was just getting started then. She used to say that she didn't know who she was sometimes, that she missed the days when it was just the three of us in our tiny house. I don't think she liked the political side of my life very much. She died before I ever found out." His eyes misted over, and he reached for his pipe and carefully lit it.

"Yes, that is it exactly, Dad! I don't have an identity! Yes, I'm your daughter and yes, I'm Alec's fiancée, but who am I? The me inside? What do I contribute as a person? Oh, Dad, I want to do so much more than be a social butterfly! I want to be known for *my* accomplishments and not for my beauty or knowledge of the social graces. I wish I were an artist like Uncle Jake! If only I could concentrate on my art work and be known for it instead of as Senator Sheffield's daughter, or Alec Clarke's wife. I've got to find out who I am before I end up molded into what Alec thinks I should be. I want to go to Bermuda for a few weeks. Do you think I'm crazy and ungrateful?"

Her father smiled and shook his silver head. "No, honey, I don't. I think we expect too much of you, and you always give without complaining. Alec and I are to blame. You should get away from all this confusion. I approve heartily! It's the least we can do for you—give you the time to get yourself together. Alec agrees, doesn't he?" He watched his daughter thoughtfully.

Lindsay smiled and shook her head. She shrugged her shoulders and murmured, "No, Dad, I'm afraid Alec does not understand. But then, I've come to the realization that it's more important that I follow my own thinking than Alec's advice. Perhaps when I return I won't feel so uncertain of my feelings for him. At least I was right about you. I knew you'd understand and put my feelings first." She sighed and leaned over, placing her arms around her father's shoulders.

"You'll do all right, honey. Just a few days alone on those beaches and you'll straighten everything out. I'm just glad you felt you could talk to me. If anything ever comes up that you're uncertain of, you won't hesitate to talk to your old man, will you, Lindsay?" He squeezed her hands and kissed her cheek. Lindsay smiled and thought how different he was from the distinguished senator that could stir hearts on the floor of the Senate with his rigorous, independent spirit. Many of his constituents would not have believed that this warm, soft-eyed father was the same tall, dignified politician.

"I'm going to bed now, Dad. Thanks for being here."

He nodded gruffly as she turned to leave. Her last impression that night was of her father's silver head bent over his work, his pipe left unsmoked in the ashtray. As she walked up the stairs, Raymond Sheffield looked up from his paperwork and sat back in his chair, staring into space, a solemn look on his face as he concentrated once again on lighting his pipe, his daughter on his mind.

Chapter Two

Lindsay stared thoughtfully out the window of the airplane as white clouds floated swiftly by. Her vacation in Bermuda had been wonderful, as peaceful as she had hoped. And she had come to a decision that had been eating away at her for the last month.

She had sat back on the warm beach, gazed thoughtfully at the clear green-blue waters surrounding the Bermuda shore and come to a final decision, a decision that would alter her life dramatically. She would break her engagement to Alec Clarke. It was that simple. He represented everything that was becoming repugnant to her—the social whirl, the constant facade of maintaining an appearance, of smiling when she didn't wish to and, most of all, of being in the public light. She longed for a private life, and Alec would never provide her with one.

She would tell him when she returned to Washington. Perhaps he would understand, but in truth Lindsay was certain he would not, that he would be hurt and confused by her refusal to marry him. She knew he had looked forward to having her as his wife, but now she wondered if he had ever really loved her.

She frowned. That was what had been bothering her all this time. She had the deep down feeling that she was being used, manipulated. Perhaps she was just an idealistic schoolgirl, longing for the passion that women were supposed to feel when they were in love. But Alec had never set any sparks on fire when he kissed her, and she was very confused and concerned about her lack of warmth toward him. Somehow she felt it should be different, and she was afraid of being trapped in a marriage of convenience with Alec, afraid of not loving him and not being loved in return.

Lindsay now realized that she was really looking for the kind of love her parents had shared. It would not be fair to Alec to continue this charade. It must be broken off before any permanent damage was done.

She smiled slightly to herself. She was certain that her father had guessed what was the matter with her before she had left. How typical of him to allow her to think it through for herself. He was too wise to impose his own ideas on her. If the Washington social life was not for her and didn't make her happy, he would be the first to tell her to forge ahead and find out what *would* make her happy. He had always wanted what was best for her.

Her father was away this week and wouldn't be home when she returned. She had thought of phoning him, but decided she would rather tell him in person. She had decided that she wanted to study art, in particular, painting. Deep down she now admitted that it had always been her first love.

If she had been more honest with herself and Alec, she would have admitted much earlier that painting was the one thing she had always wanted to do with her life. This dream had not been realized because of the sudden death of her mother when she was twelve. Her father had become concerned with the lack of a woman in his life. Realizing that his increasingly busy career would not allow him to devote much time to his daughter, he had decided to enroll Lindsay in the finest European schools available, where she had learned dance, languages, and culinary skills. She had complied with his wishes because he felt this was the best thing for her. She would have done anything to make him happy.

She was molded into a perfect product of her generation, able to communicate in many languages with ease, to intelligently converse with strangers on any subject, and to dress well, and arrange her hair stylishly. She was taught how to walk, talk, and dine gracefully.

Her benefactors had taken a slightly plump, young, and frightened girl and produced a coolly calm and mature young woman of the world, a true sophisticate. This, she felt, when she calmly returned home at the age of eighteen, her head held high, was what her father had wanted, what he had paid for and what he had received.

Lindsay had arrived prepared to assume her position in her father's frantic and sometimes confusing world of politics. In hoping to please him she had become an intelligent and beautiful asset, and he was pleased and proud that she had chosen to take her place at his side. It would have been a difficult position for any young woman of eighteen, but then Lindsay had a natural sophistication that offered itself naturally to the frantic and important social events to which her father was invited.

Lindsay had taken after her mother in appearance. But perhaps her most striking feature was her eyes. Whenever people met her for the first time, their eyes were immediately drawn to her face. She had her Irish mother's fine, clear white skin and her eyes were a clear and sparkling turquoise. Her hair was as black as a raven, with blue-black highlights, and was naturally parted in the center, falling softly to her shoulders. She had a tiny nose that tilted up and a firm chin, a sign of determination and strength. She was known for her beauty, although she tended to take her good looks for granted.

Lindsay was very popular and had many dates, most of them eligible, wealthy bachelors in Washington. Many had been surprised when she had chosen the young and handsome aide, Alec Clarke. And perhaps they were right when they noted that Lindsay had chosen the up and coming Alec Clarke because her father approved of him as a future son-in-law.

Yes, she had beauty, wit, vitality and was completely

unhappy. Well, she thought with determination, she would see what she could do about straightening out her life. She would talk to Alec and convince him that this was the best for both of them.

As she walked through the airport and out into the now crisp fall air, Lindsay saw Emerson walking toward her, a welcoming smile on his face. She glanced behind him. He had brought her own car, a bright red Porsche Targa, and he wasn't dressed in his usually severe uniform.

"Bless you, Emerson!" she cried. "What made you think of bringing my car instead of the limousine? And you look so sporty in your outfit!" She grinned at the self-conscious look on his usually dignified face.

"Well, Miss Lindsay, I am fully aware of your attitude toward the unwarranted gossip in the papers, and realizing that your absence during the last two weeks would not go unnoticed, I naturally assumed the reporters would be on the lookout for your arrival, and would therefore watch for the family limousine. Hence, I assumed that they would not notice your own automobile. Here, miss, allow me to help you with those canvases. I see you did some painting while you were away."

Emerson carefully laid Lindsay's art supplies in the back jump seat and placed her suitcase in the front trunk. Lindsay slipped into the front seat and lovingly slid her fingertips over the smooth leather wheel. This was her only indulgence, this bright red sports car. In it she could take off and leave her cares behind her, allowing the cool wind to tear unrestrained through her long hair. She smiled as Emerson gingerly maneuvered himself into the front seat beside her, his long legs bent under his chin. Lindsay laughed with pleasure. Emerson had never looked so undignified.

As Lindsay sped toward home, Emerson spoke quietly. "Mr. Clarke called and left a message for you, miss. I assured him I would give it to you as soon as I saw you. He asked me to relay that he wouldn't be able to pick you up at the airport and that he will be out of town for a few days. He will see you at home the night of the dinner party that you are giving for him, if that is convenient. That was all, miss."

Lindsay noted with some amusement that Emerson seemed put out. With a slight hint of sarcasm, she smiled and raised one dark eyebrow. "What's the matter, Emerson? Disappointed that my dear fiancé neglected to pass on a word of love? Don't be. I'm certainly not."

Emerson quickly glanced at this dark girl, for whom he had deep affection. She certainly didn't seem put out at Mr. Clarke's lack of affection! Something very strange was going on here.

Lindsay pulled into the driveway and parked the car at the back of the house, leaving everything but her suitcase in the car. "I'll get my painting things later, Emerson. I'll carry my suitcase upstairs myself, thanks. And thanks again for picking me up; you're a lamb!" Her long legs swiftly carried her into the cool house and up the stairs to her room.

Once inside, she quickly took off her shoes and lay down on the bed in the darkened room, her thoughts rambling. Perhaps it was better that she wouldn't see Alec until the party. It would better prepare her for what she had to say. If she told him ahead of time, she knew he would sulk throughout the evening. Lindsay realized that Alec was probably in love with the image that she had created. She would have nothing more to do with it. She had done enough and was determined to go her own way and to do the things in life she loved most. She wasn't a city girl; she loved the country and missed it.

She wanted to return to the painting that she had begun in Europe. She loved to be by herself, away from the crowds and noise, and at one with the sun and sky and earth. She felt now that she had been as guilty as Alec in assuming the role he had created for her. She intended to put a stop to it immediately, before it got out of hand. She was not the girl that Washington felt she was—a great party girl, always ready for a good time, always anxious to attend any social function and to have her beautiful face appear in the newspapers. She was deeply ashamed of this false image and more and more resentful of Alec's use of her social talents. She would go somewhere else where people would not know Lindsay Sheffield, the Senator's daughter, Alec Clarke's fiancée, that girl from the Washington social whirl.

The night of the party Lindsay continued to play hostess for Alec, smiling coolly and looking beautiful in her backless black crepe gown, which clung to her breasts and hips. Her shoulder length hair, gleaming blue-black, swung down to her creamy shoulders.

She would do her best as hostess for Alec this one last time, she thought. He had arrived just before the first guests and seemed worried and preoccupied. After a quick kiss, he had walked quickly over to the bar and poured himself a stiff drink, downing half of it in one gulp. Before Lindsay could ask what was wrong, the first guests had arrived and she had been forced to leave him.

For most of the evening Lindsay watched Alec from the corner of her eye wondering at his dark mood. He seemed to avoid her and frequented the bar constantly.

As she turned to leave the couple she had been conversing with, she noticed a man watching her. She inwardly cringed, instinctively not liking the way he looked at her, his eyes traveling up and down the length of her body. Lindsay knew he was a well-known reporter that Alec had invited to the party despite her protest, insisting that he could help his career enormously. Well, she thought, she would be polite and a good hostess, interested in the well-being of her fiancé's guests. Alec would have to be satisfied with that.

She didn't understand how this man could be so important to Alec. His suit was wrinkled and much too small for his overweight frame. His face had a dissipated look as if from too much alcohol and late nights. He actually leered at her. He was in for a big surprise if he thought she was the playgirl that the other newspapers had built her up to be.

He walked toward her, a drink in one hand and a large,

foul-smelling cigar in the other. He nodded and pointed to the room full of people. "My name is Joe Pearson," he said. "You've heard of me?" His small eyes seemed to pin Lindsay to the floor.

She lost her smile and quietly nodded. This man was not just any reporter. He could create scandal out of the most innocent words. She hated the man and all he stood for. How could Alec have anything to do with this creature?

Suddenly remembering her good manners, Lindsay smiled stiffly. "I hope you're enjoying yourself, Mr. Pearson."

"I am, honey, I am, and I intend to do so much later in the evening, after the party, if you know what I mean?"

Lindsay stared at him, trying to keep her dislike from her calm voice. "I'm afraid I don't, Mr. Pearson."

He started to laugh loudly, then whispered, "You sure do maintain a cool image, Lindy, I'll give you that! You damn well do know what I'm talking about. Your boyfriend talked to you, didn't he?" His lips sneered as he gestured in Alec's direction. Lindsay could see Alec's cold eyes taking in the reporter.

She slowly led him across the room, smiling graciously to people as she passed them, until she had entered a smaller, more private room. Leaving the door open slightly, she turned abruptly and said sharply, "Now perhaps you'll be good enough to tell me what this is all about? You are Alec's guest, not mine, Mr. Pearson, and I'm not used to the rude behavior you exhibit!"

He grinned, gazing deliberately down her body. She looked back at him and said coolly, "My name is Lindsay, not Lindy, and despite whatever impressions the Washington newspapers or my fiancé have given to you, I do not like rude people and I do ask them to leave my parties, as quickly as possible. Do I make myself clear, Mr. Pearson? Shall I call Emerson to escort you to the door? I'm sure you are ready to leave by now."

He glanced at her shrewdly and slowly smiled, nodding to himself. "Are you aware, Miss Sheffield, that I have obtained certain information about your fiancé, information that if printed by me could ruin his political future and at the same time smear your father's name? If you refuse to cooperate with me, tomorrow's papers will carry all the unsavory details about your fiancé's recent activities."

Lindsay stared at him, horrified, her face suddenly paling. She felt the leering eyes of this stranger watching her with confidence. What had Alec done that could give this man such power over him? How could it affect her father? She knew her father to be an honorable and just man.

Lindsay pulled the door closed and turned quietly toward Joe Pearson. She was determined not to lose her anger until she knew what this was all about.

"What do you want, Mr. Pearson, and what can Alec have done that could possibly affect my father's good name?" She remained calm and cool.

He chuckled. "I notice you seem more concerned about your father than you do about your fiancé, Miss Sheffield. Interesting. Perhaps Alec Clarke is wrong, and you won't come to his aid, eh?"

"What does Alec think I will do for him, Mr. Pearson?"

Pearson's eyes sharpened and he said tersely, "Why, pay off his gambling debts, Miss Sheffield. To the tune of four thousand dollars. You see, Miss Sheffield, Alec has been losing regularly at private card games. You look surprised. I can see now that you weren't aware that your Prince Charming had some faults, some very expensive faults. He's been using the Sheffield name as collateral and now I'm here to collect. I have the I.O.U.'s right here, Miss Sheffield. Either way I get a story. You pay off the debts, as Clarke said you would, he'll quietly resign from your father's staff, and I'll get the scoop. If you refuse to pay off the debts, he'll still owe them to certain individuals and I'll print the story. Your father's name won't be absolutely clear, will it? After all, Alec Clarke is his future son-in-law and he trusts him. That won't look good to the people who voted for your father, will it?"

Lindsay felt sick. This man would do as he said. She

had no alternative if she was to protect her father. Joe Pearson would never believe her if she told him the engagement with Alec was off. Nor would he care. A story was all that mattered to him.

"May I see the I.O.U.'s, Mr. Pearson? I assume all of them are here?" she asked calmly. He nodded abruptly, placing a pocketful of papers in her outstretched hand. Lindsay quickly added up the figures. Some were dated as far back as six months. Alec must have foreseen this and asked her to marry him as protection. He was not only ambitious, but she could now see that he was coolly calculating as well. She smiled bitterly, knowing that Alec was perfectly aware she would do anything to protect her father.

Lindsay walked over to the desk and withdrew a checkbook. She scribbled across the check, quickly signed it, and handed it to Pearson. He took it eagerly, smiling with satisfaction.

"This should do it, Miss Sheffield. Clarke's creditors will be satisfied and your father will be protected." He studied her with admiration. "What are you going to do with poor Alec, now that you've discovered he has a few faults? What happens the next time he runs up a few debts?"

Lindsay glared, her head held high. "There won't be a next time, Mr. Pearson," she said sharply. She folded the I.O.U.'s neatly and walked over to the desk. Without looking up, she spoke huskily. "The situation is this, Mr. Pearson. If one word of anything that would be detrimental to my father's career appears in any newspaper syndications, I will use my father's influence to thoroughly discredit you. If I have to, I'll tell anyone who will listen that you blackmailed me tonight. I'll have the cancelled check with your name on it as proof. My father is well respected across the country. I think you should leave now." She smiled politely at him. His face was beet red with anger, and he seemed ready to explode as he turned and walked slowly to the front door. As Emerson opened it for him, he turned and looked back at Lindsay, her head held high, her chin up in the air and her eyes flashing with blue-green lights. "You're Sheffield's daughter, all right!" he said, and walked through the door.

Emerson closed the door and turned to Lindsay. Her shoulders had suddenly drooped, and her face was sad. "Are you all right, Miss Lindsay?" he asked.

She looked up at him, her lilting voice soft, and said, "I will be from now on, Emerson, thank you. Would you come with me to the study? I want you to give Mr. Clarke a note."

Lindsay walked over to the desk and wrote a brief note to Alec, enclosing the I.O.U.'s. Withdrawing the ring from her finger, she quickly dropped it into the envelope. She wrote a second brief note to her father explaining what had happened, and saying that she was going away for a while to escape the newshounds that would inevitably follow her after Alec's resignation. She smiled grimly as she handed the envelope to Emerson.

Her father would respect her need for privacy. She would let him know where she was later. As she walked out of the study and up the stairs to her bedroom, she thought of Alec and shook her head in pity. Emerson would just now be telling him that she had retired early because of a headache. But would he believe it? He wouldn't read her note until Emerson gave it to him after the party. A smile came to her lips as she thought of what she had written. "Dear Alec: I thought I was worth more than four thousand dollars. The party's all yours. Goodbye, Lindsay."

Chapter Three

Lindsay went to her closet and took out a pair of denim jeans, a shirt, and a heavy pull-over sweater. She picked up her tennis shoes, heavy socks, and a change of underclothes and slipped them into a small carryall with her hairbrush and sunglasses. Grabbing her leather day purse, she quickly looked for the money left over from her holiday in Bermuda. She hadn't had a chance to redeposit it in her checking account. She had about twelve hundred dollars left. She left her checkbook on her vanity. She wouldn't be able to use it where she was going. The townspeople might recognize her name and Washington address and notify the local press.

Lindsay slipped off her evening slippers and put on a pair of crepe-soled clogs. Her painting equipment and canvases, including new brushes and paints that she had just purchased, were all in her car. She hadn't had time to bring them into the house, thank goodness. She glanced around her room, not wanting to take the time to gather anything else that she might need. She would buy supplies and other clothes when she reached her destination.

By now Alec would be looking for her, wondering why she had not returned to the party. If she could sneak down the servants' back stairs and out the back door, she could reach her car and leave immediately. She could make it to

Vermont by noon the next day if she drove almost contin-
uously.

Lindsay slipped down the back stairs without being noticed, walked quickly to her car, and drove away. No one
saw her leave.

At three thirty the next morning Lindsay suddenly felt
tired as she realized the enormity of what she had done.
Needing a brief rest, she parked her car in a highway rest
area and walked around, moving her arms to lessen their
stiffness. Despite her driving gloves, her fingers felt stiff
too.

She thought of where she was headed—a place out of
her past where no one would recognize her. The idea had
come to her a month before when she had received a letter from her Uncle Jake, who owned a cabin in the great
wooded area just beyond the Vermont–New York border.

He wasn't really her uncle. He was a famous painter
presently traveling in Greece for a few months. He and
her parents had been close friends while she was growing
up, and she remembered how as a child of ten she and
Jake had gone fishing, mountain climbing and apple picking in October, when the fall leaves had started to change
color from green to glorious red, yellow, and bright
orange. Even the air had smelled fresher—different somehow. No place on earth compared to this land in southern
Vermont.

Her parents had come to Vermont each fall, but one
fall season in particular had left its impression forever on
the budding painter in young Lindsay. Uncle Jake had noticed her growing love for the land and even then had felt
that, given the training and the chance, she would become
a great artist. But her mother's sudden death and her sub-
sequent schooling in Europe had brought an abrupt end to
his dreams.

Lindsay's father and Jake had gone to college together
and remained friends even after her mother's death.
Lindsay had thought that Jake, a widower, had once loved

her mother in his younger days. Perhaps that was why he always treated her like the daughter he had never had.

He did have a son, though—Jason Mainwaring, who had always been away at college. He would be about thirty-three now, she mused. Funny, in all the years they had gone to the cabin, she only met Jason a couple times. He was studying architecture and was always away either at school or visiting a foreign country to study architecture.

Jake had always spoken proudly of how well Jason had done in school and how many architectural firms were interested in him. Jason's mother had been part Indian, which, according to his father, accounted for his dark good looks. Jake jokingly swore that sometimes when Jason and he were out camping or fishing, he would change into an Indian. His love of nature and his father's artistic eye had directed him toward a career in architecture. Jake had quietly boasted that Jason always designed buildings composed of natural elements, like redwood and cedar, with pure, open spaces bounded by huge expanses of glass. He told his father that people were too imprisoned in their cement-block houses. They needed to escape from the noise of the cities and the stresses of their jobs by finding peace in a quiet wooded house designed with nature's help and compliance.

Lindsay knew from having heard Uncle Jake's tales of Jason's escapades that he was a very dark man with pitch black eyes and thick black hair. He had taken after his mother with his strikingly dark, hawkish good looks. She also remembered that Jason Mainwaring was said to be quietly private, like his father.

Lindsay smiled slightly as she recalled how many times Jake had sat chuckling with delight as he read the latest newspaper account of his son's social life in Europe. Jason had been no saint and probably could choose any woman he wanted. It was said that he hated personal appearances and parties, and only went to Europe to design a house upon special request. Immediately upon completing it, he flew back to his home in the Vermont woods.

Lindsay shook her head slightly and thought how strange it was that she should know so much about Jason even though she hadn't seen him in years.

She stretched her slim arms, reached into the car, and removed a folded letter from her glove compartment. It had come from Jake a month ago. He had invited her to come up to the cabin that she had found such pleasure in as a child. He had frequently read about her in the papers and had been as displeased as she to find her name there constantly. He had offered her the use of the cabin since he would be in Greece painting the magnificent Aegean Sea and the surrounding islands. He had not mentioned Jason, and Lindsay sighed softly as she concluded that after all these years Jason must be married with a family of his own.

The bright red Porsche raced onward as Lindsay drove with determination, suddenly downshifting to maneuver a sudden sharp turn. She had been driving fast all night, trying to arrive in Vermont before someone recognized her. She was now passing over the Tappan Zee Bridge near New York on the Hudson. Soon she would be past the heavily populated sections of the metropolitan area.

Few people would notice a beautiful, dark-haired girl driving a sports car, especially near New York City, but if daylight came quickly and she hadn't traveled far enough north and away from "civilization," someone might remember her distinct red Porsche and the slightly familiar face of the young woman driving it.

If her picture appeared in a paper all the way up here, anyone—a gas station attendant, a waitress in a diner, or a state policeman—might recognize her, and phone a paper with the story for the chance of getting their own name in the paper.

Lindsay felt tired again. Her foot was stiff. She had been careful to keep her speed down to the maximum limit on these super-highways, but it had now been five hours since she had left the Washington party in her father's brownstone. She stifled a yawn.

She was approaching an empty rest area. She downshifted and maneuvered her Porsche into a grassy plot facing the rising sun. This far south it was still too early for the beautiful fall colors to have appeared. They would soon create a natural painting that could never be perfectly recreated from an artist's palette.

Lindsay glanced down quickly at the formal gown she was wearing and grinned. She hadn't even stopped to change her clothes. She looked around at the silent countryside. There was no traffic up here yet. She reached into the jump seat for the pair of denim jeans and the cotton shirt she had taken from her closet, and changed into them. She slipped off the clogs she was wearing and put on socks and tennis shoes. Now she wouldn't be quite as noticeable when she went to town.

She'd reach Jake's cabin in about five more hours at the most. It was located just outside Bennington, Vermont, which could supply her with food and clothes and anything else she might think of at the last moment. She would then be able to "hole in" at the cabin. She'd drive into the town on the way to the cabin and get everything she might need in one trip. Even way up in Bennington, where most of the residents liked to live away from larger cities, there was a chance that someone might remember the slim, dark beauty who had briefly stopped in their tiny town for a few hours. They would be sure to remember her red car, if not her face.

She lay the dress, after folding it carefully, in the back seat, then gazed at it for a moment, recalling the time when she had purchased it. It was a Dior, a perfect dress for one of Washington's most popular hostesses. Wearing it, she had made Alec proud, and had thought she had seen love in his eyes. Instead, she now realized, sadly, all she had seen was the self-love of a man who was pleased to have a perfect hostess for his politically important social gatherings.

Shrugging these thoughts aside, Lindsay slid into the front seat. She had better get moving. She would buy a cup of coffee to keep her awake when she stopped for gas.

Traffic along the Hudson Valley was starting to pick up now, but not enough to cause alarm. The farther north she drove, the thinner the traffic became and she relaxed, taking time to enjoy the changing scenery.

She saw a small restaurant on the roadside and pulled in. The attendant, not used to seeing such a beautiful girl in such a sporty car, strolled over and placed his hands on the door.

"Ma'am? Fill 'er up?" he asked, his eyes taking in the interior of the expensive car.

Smiling quickly, Lindsay nodded.

"You get good mileage with these here 911s?" he asked as he lovingly polished the windows and mirror. "Maybe you're one of those New York models, miss?"

Smiling to herself, Lindsay quickly shook her head, asking him what she owed him and handing him small bills, afraid he might remember one large bill when he made change. Then she stopped in the small coffee shop for a couple of quick cups of black coffee and a Danish pastry. The waitress had other things on her mind and didn't pay much attention to Lindsay.

She drove off slowly, but increased her speed as soon as she was out of sight. Thank God! Now she could go the rest of the way without stopping.

Lindsay knew that when her father returned home and read her note, he would tell no one that she had left Washington. Eventually her absence would be noted, especially when Joe Pearson wrote his story of Alec's resignation. Her father would wait patiently for her to phone him and let him know her whereabouts. She also knew deep down that he would approve of her leaving.

Soon she came to Troy, New York, and turned onto Route Seven, heading east toward the Vermont border. She was becoming anxious and excited despite her growing fatigue. Her mounting excitement seemed to increase the adrenaline in her body and she became more alert. It wouldn't be long now.

She looked for the sign that said New York–Vermont border. There it was! In Vermont Route Seven changed to the Molly Stark Trail. It continued eastward, a curving mountainous road.

Lindsay entered the famous town of Bennington, known for its Bennington pine furniture. She maneuvered through the town, which had grown larger than she remembered, and pulled into a parking space. This would do nicely.

She entered a shop that carried women's clothing and methodically selected casual slacks, sweaters, shirts, and a few pairs of shoes, one comfortable pair for strolling in the woods, and a slightly dressier pair of sandals. She quickly added a casual, hand-smocked peasant dress to match the sandals. A cream-colored fisherman's net heavy pullover sweater was added to the pile, and a navy peacoat for colder weather.

While the saleslady was placing her purchases in boxes, Lindsay walked next door to a men's shop and bought three large men's shirts in turquoise broadcloth to serve as painting smocks.

Throwing these purchases into the trunk, Lindsay turned to a local drug store and bought a few paperbacks, some cosmetics, shampoo, and soap. She knew Jake would have sheets, towels, and kitchen supplies at the cabin. She bought some old-fashioned flannel nightgowns because she knew how cold the nights could be. If only her friends could see her in one of those outfits, in place of the frilly lace and silk creations she usually wore!

Her last stop was at a supermarket. She stocked up on everything she might need. The cabin had quite a large freezer and a modern refrigerator, so Lindsay knew most of the bread and meats could be frozen, as well as most of the vegetables. Just to be certain in case the electricity failed, she bought canned meats, fish, and fruits as well.

After she had finished her shopping in Bennington she loaded up with gas one more time and returned to the Molly Stark Trail. About three miles down the road, to the north of the trail, was the famous Green Mountain National Forest. Jake's cabin was deep in the woods on Haystack Mountain, about a half-mile off the gravel road.

Few people were aware of the cabin's existence. The inhabitants of nearby Searsburg knew that the owner rarely showed up and that if he did, he did not wish to be disturbed. Jake had told her that they considered him "one of those strange painter fellows."

Lindsay pulled onto a tiny dirt road. Nothing had changed since her last visit except that the trees had grown taller. She looked intently ahead for the log cabin. There it was, the size of a modest house, but cozy and old-fashioned.

Lindsay parked near the front step, quickly jumped out, and ran up the steps to the door. It was locked, of course. Jake would never turn anyone away, but was afraid that a large animal from the nearby woods would get in and wreak havoc inside.

Grinning, Lindsay reached behind a tiny opening on the bottom step and pulled out a key. Nothing had changed!

She opened the front door and stepped inside. The living room was the same; nothing had been moved. It was almost as if someone lived here all the time. She went into the big kitchen, which had been expanded to accommodate the large number of people who were always at Jake's laughing, relaxing, and having a good time. Checking the freezer and refrigerator, she was surprised to find them still plugged in, the motors running. Perhaps Jake had forgotten to unplug them. She was too tired to figure it out.

She moved her things into the cabin as quickly as she could. Once all the food was put away, she piled the boxes of clothing she had bought into the spare bedroom since she would be the only one here. In the third bedroom she unloaded her canvases and painting supplies. The light was particularly bright in that bedroom, there might be days when she would prefer to paint inside.

Exhausted by now, Lindsay walked into Jake's bedroom and pulled the dust cover off the bed. It would have to be aired and remade. She checked the linen closet and found sheets and towels as well as blankets. Suddenly she remembered her car sitting out front. If anyone—a park ranger, or a lost stranger—should see it . . . She raced out and, taking the house key, drove the car to the garage that was set back in the woods about two hundred feet down the road. Jake had not wanted to look out the windows of his mountain retreat and see cars and a large garage, so he had built it away from the house.

She unlocked the garage doors and parked the car in the garage. There was no way anyone on this earth would ever see that red sports car now! She closed and locked the doors and started back to the house, feeling more and more exhausted. By the time she reached the house, it was growing colder.

She turned up the heat only a little bit because the sun was still shining into the windows and warming the room. Lindsay sat down on the huge sofa in front of the fireplace. She would make the bed in a few minutes, after she had rested her tired legs and stiff neck. She pulled a pillow more comfortably under her neck and raised her legs up on the sofa. She lay there, staring up at the ceiling and felt her eyes slowly close. She thought she heard a bird chirping right outside the window and gave a soft sigh as she fell into a sound sleep.

Chapter Four

━━━━━━━━━━━━━━━━━━━━━━━━━━━━━━━

Jason Mainwaring stopped his Mercedes in front of the cabin. It was dark, and he wanted to check the house before he returned to his own home near Lake Raponda. He usually checked the cabin a few times a week and occasionally stayed there when he had been out in the woods all day hiking or fishing. It was easier to sleep in the spare bedroom than to drive all the way home. The bed was always made up for him and he usually carried extra food with him.

Stepping out of the car slowly, he suddenly stopped and listened carefully. Something was different but he couldn't put his finger on it. He bent his ear, as if listening for any noise different than the usual night sounds in the woods around him.

Everything seemed normal, yet he couldn't shake the impression that something was amiss. Softly, like a dark panther, he tread up the front steps.

The full moon shone down on him, his straight black hair gleaming, his black eyes glittering. His skin was the darkly tanned skin of a man who spent a lot of time outdoors, and was also the result of the proud mixture of his half-Indian mother and his Cornish father.

Stepping to the door, he slowly turned the knob. The door was unlocked, yet it hadn't been forced open. He stepped down and felt for the hidden key. It wasn't there! Someone had taken the key, obviously knowing its hidden location, and at this late hour was probably inside sound asleep. It was probably one of his father's fishing cronies. Jason turned to leave.

He stopped. If it were someone he knew, then why hadn't he locked the front door upon retiring? Frowning now, Jason moved his tall, lean body lithely up the steps and quietly opened the door.

The living room was dark. He heard nothing, and saw no movement. He stalked, catlike, across the main living room into the master bedroom. Black eyes squinted in the moonlight and, with the clear eyesight of a cat, surveyed the room. The bed had been stripped but nothing was missing from the room.

He turned abruptly and paced across to his room. On his bed lay several boxes containing what was obviously clothing. He recognized the names of Bennington stores on the boxes and bags.

Slowly picking up the lid of one box, he took out the garment inside and examined it. It was a man's shirt, quite a large one from the size on the label. He frowned and opened another box, this one from an exclusive woman's shop. Pulling out a long, feminine gown, he noted that it was a casual lounging robe. He was not a novice when it came to women's clothing. He looked over the bed carefully, trying to ascertain who his visitors were. They were obviously out right now, yet they were familiar enough with the cabin to know where his father hid the key.

Jason laughed silently when he came upon the flannel nightgowns, the only sleepwear he found. Marcia would never have been seen in one of these. She usually preferred a more sophisticated transparent chiffon gown for sleep. He frowned again. There was no consistency here. There were exactly three men's shirts, all the same color, and the rest of the clothes were all a woman's. Whoever had come here had not planned any social outings, that was certain.

He walked into the third bedroom and stared at the

canvases and paints. These didn't belong to his father. He hadn't seen them here last week when he had stopped in.

He checked the kitchen and opened the refrigerator and freezer. They were stocked with food, enough for quite a few weeks. Perplexed, he shook his head. If anyone had been coming here to stay, they would have phoned him. He didn't like puzzles. He was used to being in complete control of any given situation. His work was proof of that. He designed a house the way he felt it should look in its natural surroundings and his plan was either accepted or he refused the contract.

The same went for Marcia Headley. She accepted their arrangement for now, knowing that he refused to be tied down by marriage. She had class and beauty and he had a good time with her, but he would not allow her to interfere in his life, especially when he chose to be by himself in the woods.

Jason grinned to himself. How Marcia hated this cabin. She couldn't stand anything stuffy and old, anything that spoke of the past, and she refused to come with him whenever he stopped by.

He walked into the living room to wait. He would start a fire and just sit. He walked quietly over to the fireplace in the dark, knowing his way by heart, and slowly placed twigs and logs in the fireplace with a minimum of effort. He bent over and lit the fire, the now flickering flames softening the angular planes of his hawkish face.

Picking up a burning twig, Jason lit a cigarette. He sat crouched in front of the fire until he was sure it would continue to burn, then he added one more log and stood up, stretching his long frame. He turned to the sofa behind him and stopped abruptly, staring at the picture before him.

The firelight flickered softly over the face of a beautiful girl, who lay curled up in a ball with her tiny feet drawn up under her. Her fragile face lay half hidden in a soft pillow which she clutched in her arms, her dark lashes fanning over white cheeks. Her long black hair, parted in the middle, tumbled in soft disarray down the side of her face and onto the pillow.

Jason took in the soft curves of her breasts and hips, and the tiny span of her waist. Despite the fact that she wore rough denims, he could tell that her long legs were slim. She looked like a lost child lying there, and he noted that she was shivering slightly. He took a blanket from a nearby chair and stood over her, watching her as she slept, totally unaware of his presence. She seemed unafraid and secure on the sofa, and also at peace. She slept the sleep of the innocent. He smiled to himself and gently draped the blanket over her.

She gave a tiny smile, as if feeling the blanket's warmth, and pulled it more closely about her. He noted that she wore no wedding band. He also abruptly realized something else: he had seen this girl somewhere before. Her slight smile had jogged a memory. Where had he seen that smile before? Her face was still partially hidden by her hair and the pillow, yet he knew he had seen her somewhere.

He lit another cigarette and squinted through the smoke. Shaking his dark head in frustration, Jason watched her closely for any sign of awakening, and finally decided that she was much too tired. She would probably sleep through the night.

He looked around the room. There were no suitcases, or any other evidence of a man staying with her, despite the three shirts he had found in his room. He knew they couldn't be a present for his father because they were much too large. Whom did they belong to? How had she gotten here? Had someone dropped her off with all her packages and that enormous supply of food? Would that person return during the night? She was obviously not a runaway because the clothes and food had cost a lot of money. He stood deeply in thought, trying to unravel the puzzle.

If she had a car of her own, and knew where the key to the cabin was, then there was a good chance she also knew that the key would fit the garage door as well. Jason grabbed a flashlight from the shelf and walked out the door, closing it partially to prevent awakening her.

He strode down to the garage and stared into the window. Yes, there was her car. He opened the doors and stepped inside, flipping on the overhead light. Running his long fingers through his thick hair, Jason whistled softly. He stared at the expensive car, its bright red color glaring from beneath the garage light bulb. He sighed deeply, letting his breath out slowly.

Whoever this girl was, she obviously had money but since she had only brought casual clothes with her, it would seem that she planned on staying near the cabin. And as tired as she had been, she had taken the time to hide the car in the garage and then carefully lock it. Jason looked at the license plate. Washington, D.C., it read. He stared at it, a slightly sardonic smile coming to his firm lips. Then he nodded to himself. Now he knew where he had seen the girl before. He had seen that smile not long ago in Ray Sheffield's home. The girl lying on his sofa was no other than Lindsay Sheffield, and her picture had been placed on a table in the foyer of the Sheffield home.

Jason stood in the glaring light, his fingers resting on his slim hips, a puzzled frown on his dark face. Why had Lindsay Sheffield come to the cabin? If she had planned a vacation here, she would have contacted him in Jake's absence and asked if it would be convenient. Apparently she shared his father's love of painting, hence the canvases and painting supplies in the third bedroom.

Wait a minute! She couldn't have contacted him because she quite obviously didn't know he had anything to do with the cabin. Perhaps she didn't even know he lived around here. That explained why she had placed all those boxes and bags on his bed. Lindsay had no way of knowing he used the cabin and had his own bedroom there.

Jason pulled the light cord and stood in the dark, thinking, trying to unravel the puzzle of Lindsay Sheffield and why she had come into his life so suddenly. She must have driven straight here from Washington, judging from how tired she was. She had fallen asleep on the sofa without even a blanket to cover her. Why the rush?

Jason thought again of her quiet beauty as she lay on the sofa sleeping. He had seen her only twice in his life, both times when she was just a child. He smiled. She was certainly no child now!

He had known a great many beautiful women all over the world, and his conquests had come easily to him. He wasn't immodest about this fact. He just accepted it and shrugged it off. Women were apparently attracted by his good looks and were willing to sacrifice anything for his attention. He had grown bored with them.

But this girl seemed different. Even in sleep he sensed that Lindsay was special. To have come all the way from Washington in a moment's notice, as it appeared to him she had done, had taken intelligence and coolness and a certain amount of recklessness. She looked eighteen at most, and yet had been able to handle whatever it was that made her leave Washington in such a hurry. Jason wondered if her father was aware of her departure.

He would just have to wait until she woke up for her explanation. He locked the garage doors, then walked back to the cabin.

Firelight filled the living room with warmth, and shadows danced on the walls. He loved the room like this. He felt most at home here, away from the city and away from social obligations. He grinned as he thought of the few choice words Marcia would have said to him if she saw the scene before him now.

A mysterious sleeping beauty on the sofa, alone with him, and a warm fire going. He stirred restlessly as he looked at Lindsay, feeling uneasy with emotions long buried. She lay there completely unprotected. If strangers had entered the cabin while she was sleeping, she wouldn't have had a chance against them. No one knew she was even here.

Jason smiled wryly to himself. He wasn't certain she would be safe from him if she continued to lie on the sofa like that. She had pushed the blanket down after feeling the warmth of the fire and her top buttons had come undone in a restless moment. The hollow of her neck, and the slight curve of her full breasts, now slightly revealed, disturbed him. He felt like bending over and kissing her awake. He wanted to feel the touch of her heavy hair under his hand and to see what color her eyes were.

She had pale white skin, black hair and eyebrows, and long black lashes. Her eyes were probably blue, as blue as the azure seas of Greece. Jason continued to muse over her. Even in sleep she bore the markings of more class and culture than Marcia could ever hope to attain. This girl in her sleep was the essence of innocence whereas Marcia had long ago lost hers. Lindsay apparently shared his father's love of nature and painting, whereas Marcia loved the social whirl, and would prefer to meet a famous painter rather than lose herself in his work.

Out of the corner of his eye Jason saw a piece of white paper lying on the floor near Lindsay's purse. It had never occurred to him to look through her purse. If she were a friend of his father's, he would have been too embarrassed and ashamed to do that. He had felt he would hear the truth from Lindsay when she awoke.

Jason bent over and unfolded the paper, noting his father's hastily scribbled note to the girl. He smiled with satisfaction. He read and then reread the note. Jake must have kept in touch with Ray Sheffield and Lindsay for these many years.

Just then he heard Lindsay stir. He refolded the note and placed it in her purse on the floor. He walked over and crouched beside her, Indian style, staring into her face.

Lindsay felt warm and secure. She was trying to fight off the hunger that was now gnawing at her stomach. She realized that she must have fallen asleep. Her eyes were facing the fire—what fire? Who had started a fire while she slept? She took in the blanket that covered her and noted the unbuttoned top of her shirt which exposed the curve of her breasts. Her fingers quickly reached to button them and stopped in mid-air. Lindsay's eyes widened.

There before her crouched a darkly handsome man with coal back eyes intently watching her. A half-smile appeared on his hawkish face.

Her turquoise eyes darkened in fear and she let out a gasp. Lindsay quickly glanced around the room as if to escape from this man who continued to watch her, now with a stoic, unreadable look on his face. He stood up and looked down at her from a great height, making her even more afraid. She trembled and instinctively pulled the blanket up to her chin.

As she forced herself to look up and meet his eyes, she let out a cry of disbelief. "You! What are you doing here!" Her eyes took in the long frame of the man who had been talking to Emerson in her father's house, the man unknown to her. He stood quietly, his arms folded as he studied her.

With a slight quirk of amusement twitching his firmly compressed lips, he answered with a slightly mocking and deeply husky voice, "That's funny. I was just about to ask you the same question. I hope you've been comfortable. I always like my guests to make themselves at home if I'm delayed, especially if they're as lovely as you."

Lindsay frowned. For some reason she had the distinct impression that this stranger was laughing at her. In her growing anger, she lost the fear that she had felt before. With lips held in a tight line, she answered tautly, "Well, I'm not your guest so you can quit looking so smug. I've been invited here by the owner, Jake Mainwaring. Who are you and what do you mean by sneaking in here and scaring me half to death?"

A sudden coolness hid the fiery burn of black eyes as he straightened and answered softly, "I'm Jason Mainwaring and I hardly think I'm intruding in my own cabin."

At his words, Lindsay cried out a trifle breathlessly, "Jason!"

As he nodded abruptly, firelight reflected off his dark face. So this was Jason, the man who preferred nature to city life. He didn't appear to be threatening her, but rather seemed to be awaiting an explanation as to who she was and why she was here. What an idiot she was! Jason was the dark stranger whose saturnine good looks had kept her awake many nights after she had first seen him that day. It had been Jason all along, and she hadn't even known it. She had not even questioned her father about him. She had always been interrupted when she was just about to inquire about the tall stranger. After all these years, here was Jason.

Her heart pounded violently as she realized that she had been so impulsive in her wish to arrive at the cabin, that she had never considered the possibility that Jason might be here, or that he might have guests at the cabin. How could she have been so inconsiderate and thoughtless? Embarrassment flooded her face, staining her cheeks a bright red. She bit her bottom lip, quickly met his eyes, and said softly, "I'm sorry. I've intruded. I'm Lindsay Sheffield, Jason."

He raised one dark eyebrow and answered drily, "I know, Lindsay. Your father keeps an excellent likeness of you in the foyer of your Washington home. I saw it when I stopped by a month ago. It's been a long time since I've seen you, Lindsay. You've . . . grown up." His eyes glinted with amusement and appreciation as he turned and placed another log on the burning fire.

"You know who I am? Why didn't you say so at once?" Lindsay turned to Jason as he moved the blanket aside and took a seat next to her on the sofa. His very nearness caused her to become nervous again, uncertain of herself.

He smiled at her, taking in the flushed cheeks and blazing eyes, now a deep sapphire in the darkened room. Her dark hair lay tumbled around her face in soft disarray. Placing his slim fingers behind his dark head, he lay back on the sofa and stretched his long legs out in front of the fire. He gazed reflectively into it.

Lindsay stared at his strong profile and gasped at his nonchalance. "You mean to tell me you knew immediately who I was by seeing me in a photograph? I don't believe it. You weren't in our house long enough!" She bit her tongue at her slip. Damn!

Jason chuckled. "So there *was* someone watching me that day. I thought so." He laughed at her sudden discomfiture. "Well, my imp, you deserved to be found out. Actually, your license plates helped put the pieces together. As you were sleeping, I walked out to the garage and checked on your car. I saw the Washington, D.C. plates and put two and two together and came up with you. I haven't seen you since you were a kid, but your coloring and your photograph helped. I was in Washington on business and was returning home, so I stopped in to see your father. As you know, he wasn't home and time didn't permit me to stay longer. Why didn't you come down and meet me? It would have been worth a delayed trip home." He chuckled drily and Lindsay sent him a darkening look.

"I wasn't exactly dressed for entertaining when you came, Jason," Lindsay shot out. She felt ambivalent about Jason Mainwaring. He was attractive in a rough, purely masculine way, but at the same time his arrogance was irritating. She wondered what had happened to all the poise she had so recently professed to have.

"Why did you come, Lindsay?" It was a perfectly innocent question, yet Lindsay sensed Jason's determination to find out her reasons for suddenly appearing after all these years. She glanced down at her long fingers, which were now plucking the blanket. A slight frown of concentration lined her brow as she tried to decide how much she should tell him.

She looked up at him and answered quietly, "I was long overdue for a vacation and received a letter from Jake telling me that he was going to be in Greece to paint for a few months. It was his hope and the answer to a few problems that I was having at the time for me to come up here and spend my vacation in peace and solitude. I never thought I would be intruding upon you, Jason. I thought I would be alone."

He ignored the latter part of her answer and picked up on something else. He stared at her, his eyes demanding honesty and said, his voice dangerously soft, "And what problems were you having, Lindsay, that were so immediate in nature that you came running up here on the spur of the moment?"

Lindsay caught her breath and hesitated. Jason was too astute. "I wasn't certain about my life in Washington, Jason. I'm still not sure it's the kind of existence I want, especially for the rest of my life." Not a lie, but the whole truth would have to wait. She didn't know Jason well enough and wasn't even certain he would wish to be involved by hearing about the deception that Alec had initiated.

Jason looked at her intently, taking in each word. She obviously had an inborn sense of good taste, required in a senator's daughter. Lindsay had described his father's letter almost verbatim. She apparently had told him the truth. Yet he hesitated. Something didn't ring true when this beautiful girl with the sad blue-green eyes spoke. She was leaving something out, something that troubled her greatly.

Lindsay noticed the changes in Jason's expression as he listened to her brief exchange. He believed her and that was all she could hope for at the moment. For some reason this man disturbed her. She felt something awakening in her when she looked at the wide shoulders under the cream suede shirt that was open at his neck. The fine dark hairs of his chest showed, and she took in the tightening of his thigh muscles as he straightened his long legs and stood up. He was wearing fawn and cream suede pants and the colors were striking against his dark coloring. He exuded catlike strength when he walked across the room, and now he turned to her and smiled as his eyes took in her huddled form on the sofa.

"I don't know about you, Lindsay, but I'm starving and I can see that you've stocked the refrigerator well. Let's see what we can do about you over some bacon and eggs. I hope you're a good cook. You can't get away with just being beautiful up here in the woods, you know!" He grinned and she relaxed.

Lindsay smiled softly and stood up, straightening her clothes. She walked over to him in her bare feet and stood looking up at him. Even though she was tall, she had to bend her neck to look up at him.

"Jason, did anyone ever tell you that you have your father's kindness in you?"

He seemed startled by her observation and said softly, "No, Lindsay, to the contrary. Most people think I'm an ogre, even ruthless, unless I get my own way."

She looked at him as he tilted her chin, looking closely into her eyes. "I knew you had turquoise eyes, Lindsay. I knew it all along," and he gently and lightly planted a cousinly kiss on the tip of her tilted nose.

She smiled, suddenly happy at this sign of affection, and then wondered what else Jason Mainwaring knew about her. Had he known about her engagement to Alec? Perhaps her father had told him. For some reason she wished that his kiss hadn't been quite so cousinly. His nearness made her heart pound and her breath quicken. Alec had never made her feel such emotions, but then she had never been afraid of Alec. What was there in Jason that made her sense a repressed violence under the surface. She knew for a certainty that Jason Mainwaring was as different from Alec as day from night. She suspected that he was quite capable of violence and yet he showed a controlled, almost primitive strength.

Trembling, Lindsay looked up at Jason, her lips quivering. "Do you always get what you want, Jason?"

He placed his finger softly against her cheek and looked darkly into her eyes. His own eyes flickered for a moment in the firelight. She thought for a brief moment that he was going to kiss her again, but instead he smiled to himself and said softly, "I intend to now, Lindsay, I intend to."

Chapter Five

━━━━━━━━━━━━━━━━━━━━━━━━━━━━━━━━━━━━━

Jason squeezed Lindsay's shoulders and said, "I'll start things in the kitchen. You still look tired."

At her protest he held up a restraining hand and his eyes looked blacker than ever. "Look, Lindsay, I'm more used to this cabin than you are. You haven't seen it since you were a child, so will you stop giving me a hard time? I'm starving and quite capable of cooking a fast but edible meal. Now sit down and watch. I give the orders in my father's absence, and you are my guest as well as his, understand?"

She nodded slowly and followed Jason into the kitchen. He was in complete control. She was so tired she couldn't have objected if she had wanted to, and right now she didn't feel like making Jason angry.

Lindsay didn't know Jason Mainwaring but she realized that while he was like his father in some ways, he was also very different. Uncle Jake was much more easy going and had always given her a feeling of confidence, whereas Jason was introducing emotions that were new to her and left her uncomfortable and unsure of herself. He was like black lightning. She had always been able to handle any situation when she lived in Europe and then later in Washington. She had always managed to remain cool and calm under most situations, but now, in Jason's presence, she felt like a gauche schoolgirl. She was physically aware of him as well as emotionally upset at his intrusion into the life she had thought she had planned so carefully. She had hoped to be completely alone up here in the cabin and after all the care she had taken, had been discovered at once by the one person who knew who she was, Jake's son. What would he do with that knowledge? She knew now that she should have told Jason everything. Perhaps he would have offered the sanctuary of the cabin along with his silence.

But how was she to have known what to think when she had awakened, and found Jason crouching there, staring at her with those cold black eyes in that dark, unreadable face? Jason had frightened her, and she hadn't been able to think clearly. He was obviously used to honest and quick answers, and heaven help the person who didn't answer his questions to his satisfaction!

Lindsay knew nothing about him, yet she had immediately grasped his strength and determination. He seemed unrelenting, and yes, maybe he was capable of ruthlessness if he so chose. Was this what had kept her from telling the complete truth? She was afraid of his rejection and his anger.

She sighed deeply, shaking her dark head in dismay. She should have told him, she should have! Now it was too late. Jason might resent the fact that she had not been completely truthful. Perhaps after they ate she would try to tell him. He *had* been kind so far, and perhaps she had just been frightened when she first met him and had not gauged his personality correctly. She would talk to him after she had eaten. Things wouldn't look so bleak then. She was just tired and hungry and her mind couldn't function.

She watched as Jason moved around the modern kitchen with the grace of a large panther. He was certainly as darkly handsome as one and somehow seemed out of place there. Suddenly Lindsay realized that she didn't even know if Jason was married or had a family. If he didn't live here at the cabin, where did he live? It had to be close enough so that he could come to the cabin often. The thought caused an ache that she had not felt before. It unsettled her to think that he might have a wife.

She watched as his tight thigh muscles strained against the confining legs of his suede pants and her eyes moved upward to his broad shoulders. He was totally absorbed in cooking and was so tall that he almost had to bend to avoid hitting the beamed ceiling, from which hung copper pots and pans. She smiled. Jason was cooking the bacon and eggs in an old cast iron pan, instead of one of the newer porcelain and copper pans. His primary objective was to prepare and eat a simple meal as quickly as possible, and he used the pan he was most familiar with, probably one he had used since the cabin had first been built.

The kitchen looked like something out of a decorator's manual of what the "modern" kitchen should look like. She imagined the lovely culinary masterpieces she could prepare, applying what she had learned in the French and Austrian schools she had attended.

Lindsay started suddenly as she heard the toaster pop up the freshly crisped bread. She had been daydreaming, but now, as the smell of crisp bacon and sizzling eggs wafted through the kitchen, she realized she was famished.

As Jason turned and dished out the eggs and bacon into two plates, Lindsay jumped up, grabbed the toast, and put in four more slices, realizing that the four she held in her hand would never satisfy this large man's appetite. She ran to the table and quickly buttered them as Jason grinned at her eagerness. He poured coffee, strong and black, into two mugs and sat down opposite her. He nodded to her and Lindsay quickly began to eat, unable to restrain herself any longer.

She sighed with satisfaction as she ate. This had to be the best-tasting meal she had ever eaten! Jason certainly was doing credit to his own cooking as well.

After smearing some jam on her toast, she sat back in the chair and sipped her coffee—and found Jason staring at her over the rim of his coffee mug. His black eyes glittered strangely. Linsday looked up at him and then quickly down to her plate, suddenly aware that she had eaten the complete meal in silence without a word of thanks. She started to apologize for her thoughtlessness, but Jason just grinned.

"Feel better now?" he asked. He seemed to be watching her intently, as if waiting for something.

She nodded her head vigorously, smiling and feeling more relaxed. "Thank you, Jason, I think I would have gone to bed without eating if I had been here alone."

Jason watched her steadily and Lindsay squirmed under his intense scrutiny. Now was the time to tell him about Alec and the real reason why she had left Washington in such a hurry. His face had become unreadable and Lindsay felt a sudden fear, as if she had been lured into a lion's den. What if he didn't understand and thought her a coward for running away so quickly from Alec, the press?

For some reason she couldn't understand, Lindsay didn't want this dark stranger to think ill of her, and she felt certain that his anger could be aroused quite easily. Under his surface she sensed great passion that could be awakened at any moment, that could be directed into anger at her. Lindsay knew that she couldn't afford to take the chance that Jason might send her away. He probably disliked the press as much as she did and he might resent her bringing her problem up here, intruding on the peaceful world he had created for himself. She had just rediscovered the quiet beauty of that world, and now, unexpectedly, Jason, after all those years.

She wanted to know everything about him—what had he been doing when she was growing up in Europe, and what was his life like now. She also felt a subtle change taking place in herself in his presence. She didn't want to disappoint him and didn't want him to dislike her. For some reason she was drawn to him and didn't want him to leave. He was her tie to a happier past.

What had Jason been like growing up under his father's influence? Jake would have taken time for his son. He would have taken him out, taught him the ways of nature—camping, canoeing—and Jason would have become a strong man, a man of integrity and determination. His father would have instilled in Jason all the things that he had tried to teach her in the short time they had had together when she was a small child.

Jason was years older than she, and had developed artistic skills and combined them with the aesthetic tastes that his own heritage had given him. He had become a famous architect, a purist, a lover of nature. She was also aware of the fact that Jason was no puritan. He had seen a great deal of life and, according to his father, was a cynic at heart.

Jason watched the changes flickering over Lindsay's face as she sat deep in thought. He realized that there was something deeply troubling this beautiful girl. Her eyes were sad and cloudy, no longer the clear azure they had been when they had first sat down to eat. Gone was her childlike eagerness.

He longed to reach over and brush back the long strand of raven-colored hair that had fallen over her eyebrows. Giving in to his urge, he reached over and gently tucked it behind her ear. Lindsay started slightly, and her eyes widened as she sat upright. Her lips trembled as if she was trying to form words that were rising to the surface, demanding to be said.

Jason smiled encouragingly. She wasn't deliberately being mysterious and Lindsay was too innocent to play games. She had said little about herself. He knew women well and this girl wasn't one to play verbal games with him. Given the present situation, alone in the cabin with a beautiful girl from his past, Jason was surprised at his chivalrous behavior. Lindsay was desirable and he was not unaware of his own attractiveness. And yet, he had only wanted to calm her, to protect her.

Despite her obvious breeding and class and her great beauty, which even she could not deny, he realized that Lindsay Sheffield was still an innocent and she mystified him.

He quietly murmured, "You intrigue me, Lindsay, and I must admit that it's been a long time since a beautiful woman has done that." Jason poured himself another mug of coffee and sighed. He watched as Lindsay sat there, staring at her coffee, thinking hard, as if trying to say something that needed to be said. He whispered softly, "Is there something you want to say, Lindsay? I'm a good listener." Dark eyes softened momentarily to reassure her.

Lindsay glanced at Jason and after a moment nodded. A fleeting glance of hope had passed over her face. Her decision was made.

She smiled hesitantly and then murmured quietly, "Thank you for the meal, Jason. I was starving, as you could plainly see. I made a complete glutton out of myself."

Jason smiled reassuringly. "You could use some food on that slim body of yours. It's good to see a woman eat a meal and not make the usual pretense about how she has to watch her diet constantly. It's the first time I can honestly say I've been proud of my cooking abilities, or lack of them!"

They both laughed and Lindsay relaxed. The momentary sadness was gone from her face. She looked at Jason and sighed. "Jason, there was another reason I left home to come here, and you have every right to know what it is, since I've barged in here and destroyed your privacy. You might want me to leave after you hear it." She shrugged delicate shoulders.

Jason grinned slightly, raised a dark eyebrow, and said mockingly, "It can't be that bad, and if it is, I promise not to throw you out to the wolves tonight, in any case!"

Encouraged, she continued, determined to rid herself of this burden of secrecy. "Jason, when I came home after all those years in Europe, all I could think of was what a wonderful life my father and I would finally have together. I had missed him so much while I was away, and he was so proud of me. When I stepped off that plane, I was determined to devote myself to making him happy and to be whatever he wanted me to be. I did just that. I spent the next few years at his side and, as a consequence, became . . . well, a name in my own right. I was the perfect daughter, companion, and hostess for any social event on the calendar. I had to be constantly aware of my position as Raymond Sheffield's daughter, always dressed perfectly, always saying the correct thing, etc. After a while the glamour wore off, and I began to resent anything that threw me into the limelight. I was losing any sense of identity that I had, and I was becoming subject to the whims of the influential people around me. I might have been able to retain a sense of humor about all this for my father's sake, because he understood how much I valued my privacy, but outside influences interfered. The press discovered me, and any private life that I had managed to hold onto flew out the window. I became an item."

Jason nodded in quiet understanding as she hesitated. "Go on, Lindsay. I understand so far. I've been there myself."

Chewing her bottom lip, Lindsay found herself opening up. Jason *was* a good listener, and it had been a long time since she had talked to someone who really wanted to hear what she had to say.

"Well, it got worse, of course. Dad tried to discourage the items that constantly appeared in the papers, but it finally seemed that I couldn't go anywhere without being hounded by the press. I hated it. Dad used to say it came with the job, but eventually I began to wonder if the Washington whirl was really what I wanted. I think now that I was only doing what I thought my father expected of me, but I realize that all he really ever wanted was for me to be happy."

Jason sat quietly, his arms folded across his chest, listening. "That's all your father ever wanted for you, Lindsay—to be happy. He's that kind of man. I respect him a great deal."

Lindsay smiled at Jason. "Yes, and I think that's why I allowed myself to fall in love with Alec. At least, at the time I thought it was love."

"Alec?" Jason interjected. Lindsay glanced up at him and noted that a shutter had come over his black eyes.

"Yes. Alec Clarke worked on my father's staff. We met

and it was a whirlwind courtship. I knew that Dad approved of Alec—an up and coming young politician and all that. I knew that Dad wanted me to meet someone, and so I think I allowed myself to believe that Alec was the one I wanted to spend the rest of my life with. We announced our engagement a few months ago."

"You're engaged?" Jason asked a trifle heavily and shifted in his chair.

"Not now, Jason," Lindsay replied bitterly. "That's one of the reasons I came up here so suddenly. Alec deceived my father and me. I found out about it last night and it was the last straw. I couldn't bear the thought of the field day the papers would have with the story and so I ran away. I had to go some place where no one would know me, a place where I could sit back and find out where I really wanted to go in my life. I could never have done that in Washington. Uncle Jake's letter inviting me up was a godsend. No one but Dad knows about this cabin. Who would look for me up here in the wilds? I thought it inspirational at the moment!" Lindsay gave him a wry smile.

Jason reached for his mug and sipped the coffee slowly, his eyes on Lindsay's white face.

"And this Alec—does he know you're here? And what about Ray? Didn't you talk to him before you left?"

Lindsay shook her head. "I don't know what Alec is doing and I don't care. He knows nothing of this part of my life. The only thing that ever interested him was how I looked on his arm and how charming I could be to certain people. I don't think Alec was ever really interested in my true feelings. He was only interested in my image and in what value I was to him as Senator Sheffield's daughter." Her mouth tightened in bitterness.

"And what about your feelings? You don't turn love off and on like a faucet, Lindsay. And you don't fall out of love as easily as you seem to have."

"No, I suppose you're right," she sighed. "I think I might have been receptive to the opinions of my friends when it came to Alec. I saw only what they saw—his good looks, charming personality, fantastic future, security. I don't know. I didn't allow myself to see his faults and his weaknesses until last night. It was my fault as well as his. He saw something in me that wasn't really there. We were both mistaken."

"What exactly happened last night, Lindsay? Do you feel like talking about it?" Jason scrutinized her pale face.

"Why not? It might help explain why I thought I had to get away from everything." Lindsay shrugged her shoulders and ran slim fingers through the curtain of her long hair.

As Jason listened without comment, she quickly filled him in about her trip to Bermuda and the results of the party. It wasn't as difficult to relate what had happened as she had thought it would be. It was as if it had happened to another person. When she was finished, she looked at Jason, waiting for his reaction.

He shook his dark head and frowned. "So you haven't spoken to your father yet?"

Lindsay shook her head. "I can't reach him—not until tomorrow. He's away on business. I thought I would call him in the morning and explain what happened."

Jason nodded in agreement. "Well, Lindsay, it's quite a ball of wax. I seem to remember my father telling me that you used to get in all kinds of scrapes when you were a kid. It seems you're still doing it, only the scrapes are bigger!" He chuckled to himself. "I can't say I disagree with your strong dislike of the press. I've had my own problems in that area. Your sudden departure was impulsive and a bit dangerous. You could have had an accident and no one would have known where you were, and you would certainly have gotten your father worried. It was a reckless thing to do, running away like that." He shook his head, his face dark.

Lindsay watched him as he brooded over the problem that she presented. Would he send her away? She felt sick at the thought.

"Jason, please help me. Perhaps I should have taken more time to think things over, but I really do think in the end I would have come up with the same conclusion. It's been brewing for a long time. I think Dad was aware of it. I . . . I would have come to the cabin in any case. I just didn't know you'd be here.

"Oh, I've made a mess of everything! If I stay here now after what I've told you, you might be exposed to the press if they eventually take the trouble to track me down. What a field day they'd have then! 'Senator's daughter living in the cabin owned and frequented by world-famous architect.' Oh no, I'll leave in the morning, Jason. I can't involve you in this." Tears glistened in her eyes as she looked around the room in distress. She swallowed the lump that was forming in her throat.

Jason looked at her as a faint light flickered in his dark eyes. "I'd say I was pretty well involved already. You've got to spend the night here, Lindsay. It's too late to leave, and if you did leave in the morning, someone would see you anyway. There are still fall tourists camping in the National Park. Someone is certain to see your car and recognize you. And as for my reputation—well, I've never given a damn about what other people think, so I'm not about to start now." He stood up, amusement sparkling in his eyes.

Lindsay's mouth dropped slightly as she realized what Jason was saying. She took a deep breath and whispered, "Do you mean I can stay here, Jason? You don't want me to leave in the morning?"

He arched one eyebrow and took in her huddled form. A slight smile framed his mouth as he said, "No, Lindsay, I don't want you to leave . . . in the morning. You can stay here just as you had planned. There's no reason why anyone should not think you are just a guest here—of my father's, of course. If you keep that red car in the garage, no one will see it, and right now you do not look the picture of sophisticated elegance that everyone knows you for!"

Lindsay looked down and knew what he meant. Her clothes were rumpled from her deep sleep, and her hair was a mess. Gone was the makeup and the usual look of elegance that people associated with her. She smiled, excited and happy for the first time. She could stay! Jason had understood. He was right. No one need know who she was.

"Jason, thank you." She swallowed again, her eyes shining up into his. A strange light flickered in his and black lashes suddenly veiled his expression.

"It's nothing, Lindsay. Let's just say that it's the least I could do for my little . . . cousin? Now how about going out into the living room? It's growing cool in here."

Lindsay stood up immediately and found herself trembling slightly as Jason brushed by her and took her elbow. She glanced up at his dark profile. A sudden thought squelched her happiness and she found herself asking him a question that had been pushed down into the recesses of her troubled mind.

"Jason, do you have someone waiting for you? I mean it's getting late and you've spent all this time with me. Won't someone be wondering where you are?" Her eyes anxiously turned to his.

An amused grin came to his firm lips as he stopped and looked down at her. "Why, Lindsay, if you're trying to ask me if I'm married, the answer is no! That was what you were asking me, wasn't it?"

Miserably, she nodded, her eyes downcast. She was as transparent as glass! "Yes, I didn't know," she stammered, unable to continue as he gazed at her in amusement.

"Well, now you do. Satisfied for the moment?" he whispered, laughter still dancing in his eyes. Shamefaced, she nodded.

The glints of laughter suddenly left Jason's face as he took in her unhappy face. He reached out and placed a firm hand on her shoulder, drawing her closer to him. As she gazed up at him with her clear turquoise eyes, he ran a finger over her smooth cheek, trailing it down to the base of her throat. It stopped at the throbbing pulse and rested there. Lindsay became aware of her violent heartbeat and was certain that Jason could feel it in his fingertips. His eyes went to her trembling lips, and he pulled her up against his hard body with a firmness that brooked no resistance.

Lindsay lifted her head to stare up at him in amazement, and Jason very slowly bent his dark head and tasted the honey of her soft, quivering lips, holding her own softness close to him.

Slowly, Lindsay felt her lips respond to Jason's kiss as he pulled her to him as closely as possible, until she was pressed tightly against his unrelenting hardness. The heat of his body radiated into her own, causing her to melt against him. Drawing her arms up to his shoulders, Lindsay grasped him tightly as if she were falling. He slowly and gently forced her lips apart and tasted her sweetness, savoring it. She moaned slightly as she felt Jason slide his lean, hard hands up over her back to her neck, unbuttoning the first few buttons of her blouse.

Feeling as if her body were on fire, Lindsay ached with an unfulfilled need, and tried to say his name, but realized that Jason was winning a battle that she had never even had to fight before. It was the eternal battle of man over woman and Jason was an expert. He knew just what he was doing. As Lindsay felt his hands, hard and firm, moving toward her breasts, she felt herself responding with an intensity that she had never known before. She felt herself drowning in the vortex of his passion.

Jason pressed his lips deeply into the hair at her neck and moaned deeply in his throat. With a firm hand, he reached up to her shoulders and set Lindsay away from him.

Suddenly aware of his resistance, she went limp and she realized what had almost happened. What must Jason think of her?

Straightening, Jason took a deep breath and turned toward the sofa. He let his breath out slowly, trying to calm himself. Realizing what had happened and totally blaming himself, Jason knew now that Lindsay was the innocent he had originally thought her to be and that he had almost taken complete advantage of her naiveté. Frowning and angry with himself, he turned to apologize.

Lindsay mistook the look of anger on his dark face and

found tears streaming down her cheeks as she shook her head and whispered, "I'm so sorry. Jason. I don't know what to say. I don't know what to do."

He looked at her in amazement and the look of anger disappeared from his face. He started to chuckle at her ignorance and walked over to her. Taking her firmly by both shoulders, he looked down at her intently. "Lindsay, I'm sorry. I got carried away by those wide eyes of yours and the firelight. Forgive me?"

Looking up at him, Lindsay had the distinct impression that he wasn't sorry at all, but had thoroughly enjoyed that brief moment between them.

He started to smile, as if reading her thoughts, and she couldn't help but laugh. Something new had been established between them. There was a new camaraderie between them. Jason flicked her under the chin and touched each eye gently with a light finger.

"You, young woman, are tired, and should go to bed. I'm leaving now, before I get any more ideas. Lock that door when I go, do you understand?"

Nodding, Lindsay walked him to the door. He tread lightly down the steps and turned, his fingertips resting lightly on the door of his Mercedes.

"I'll stop by again to check on you in the morning, all right, Lindsay?"

"Thank you, Jason," she said softly. He nodded abruptly, slipped into the car, and drove slowly away.

Lindsay closed the door and locked it. Smiling, she returned to the kitchen, turned out the lamp, and walked over to the fireplace to check that the embers were now just softly glowing coals and quite safe. She felt the sudden heat of the fire that had ignited between Jason and herself when he had kissed her. She had never been kissed like that in her life. Certainly not by Alec. She had forgotten herself in that kiss, and had let the power from his hard, demanding body draw away all the hurt and heartache she had felt.

She had wanted to lose herself in his arms, arms that had demanded a response from her. Arms, she thought quietly, that would have provided a protective haven if only she could have told him the truth earlier.

Sighing, she turned and walked into Uncle Jake's bedroom and made the bed with the fresh linens stored in the hall closet. She took a fast shower, too tired to take time for a scented bath, and pulled the warm flannel nightgown over her dark head. Its pink ruffles just touched her toes and she looked like a small, dark-haired child, ready for bed. Lifting the large feather quilt, Lindsay slipped between the sheets and burrowed her head into the feather pillows, falling almost immediately asleep.

She dreamed of a man in a poorly fitting suit, who grinned at her and slowly walked toward her. A cigar hung from his heavy lips. As she backed away from him, she realized she had backed into something hard, something that had grabbed her by the arms and was holding her protectively against that lean hardness. She realized that the firm fingers holding her belonged to Jason and when she turned to him, he smiled and whispered her name, then disappeared.

She woke up crying out "Jason!" and, realizing that she had been dreaming, she took a deep breath and tried to relax. This was ridiculous! Why should she cry out to Jason? She had met him only that night. Jason attracted her but she didn't want to be attracted to him. She had been hurt enough by Alec when she had given her trust and heart to him. Jason could hurt her a hundred times more powerfully than Alec ever had . . . if she let him. He was a throwback to the days when men lived off the land, forging their way and making the land yield to them, just as Jason was used to making a woman yield to him. He knew this land and could live comfortably on it, and she was used to a city life. Jason was used to women of the world, sophisticated and knowledgeable in the arts of love, and she was not of that world.

They were two contrasts in a land that had once demanded complete understanding between a man and a woman in order to ensure survival. Lindsay realized that she would never understand the man known as Jason

Mainwaring, nor should she try. She was not of his worlds, neither the sophisticated. nor the primitive. She must stop thinking about him and concentrate on the day ahead. She turned over and fell into a dreamless sleep.

Chapter Six

Lindsay shivered and snuggled more deeply into the feather quilts that covered her from the top of her head to her curled-up feet. She smiled in her half-sleep as she heard the insistent morning sounds of the birds in the trees around the cabin, demanding that she awaken. Strange, she thought, the traffic sounds she usually awoke to were missing. Even on Sunday in Washington there was the usual honking of horns and the voices calling to one another across the streets where she and her father lived.

She frowned suddenly and sat upright. She wasn't in Washington anymore. She was alone in a cabin in Vermont. That was why the noises were missing. She felt cold and drew the comforter more closely around her. The fire in the fireplace must have gone out long ago. She should have turned the heat up before she retired but she had been too tired. She'd remember tonight.

She smiled and got out of bed, grabbing her robe and fleece-lined slippers, and ran to the window. The sun was shining brightly between the trees. She looked up at those surrounding the cabin and for the first time realized that she had not had the opportunity to truly take in everything when she had arrived yesterday. She had been too tired.

Lindsay gazed at the maples and oaks. They were still

green, but here and there, the hand of nature was starting to gather together the patches of bright reds and brilliant yellows, and with a slight flick of her fingers, was sprinkling the trees with small traces of these magical colors. Fascinated, Lindsay stood there, wondering at the miracle that was constantly recreated each autumn in New England, where even the bushes and brush in the fields were painted with vibrancy. Nowhere in the world was there as beautiful a change of season, from the cool of summer greens to the warm brilliance of fall colors.

She smiled slightly. Trees in the mountains and valleys of the east coast changed their colors, but in a different manner than those in Vermont. The trees down "south," near Washington and the Pennsylvania Pocono Mountains, changed to bright golds and deep reds, but the colors were never as breathtakingly vibrant as in New England.

It was as if nature had formed a complete musical composition with trees, grass, bushes, and brush, and combined everything to bring out the brightest and best of the foliage in one grand symphony of color, with the blue sky, clear and clean, as a background. Everything changed at once, and if one was unfortunate enough not to be there for the final concert, one would miss the true meaning of autumn.

Lindsay remembered that every tree changed color at one moment in time and within one week, usually around the second weekend of October, or just before. There would be one gigantic splurge and soaring of color for the world to see and then the leaves would fall, dropping to the ground in a glittering array, as if they were large, colored snowflakes. These leaves with their bright plumage didn't dry and turn brown on the tree and then drop off. They preferred a grand death, a final moment of glory, while filled with the colors of fire and gold, they plunged to earth.

Lindsay loved the New England autumn more than any other season and pitied the people who had never experienced it as she had. She was fortunate, because once she

76

had experienced a true autumn she had known then that she would never be satisfied with one anywhere else.

Her thoughts drifted to tall, dark Jason. Was he another reason she was smiling and appreciating this morning as much as she was? She remembered his kiss and her uncontrollable response. She reinforced her decision to protect herself from Jason's astute awareness of what she seemed to be thinking and his knack for catching her unawares.

She walked over to her suitcase. It was freezing in the cabin. She grabbed a bulky green pullover sweater that accented her eyes, and a pair of denims and pulled them on quickly. Walking into the bathroom, she took in her reflection in the mirror.

She looked better than she had thought she would look this morning, after what she had gone through the day before. Her skin was clear and white and there was the pink glow of good health in her cheeks. She washed her face and patted it dry with a soft towel. Brushing her long black hair until it shone, Lindsay drew it up into a ponytail and let it hang down her back. Hesitating briefly, she ran into the spare bedroom and looked at the boxes. Grabbing a blue ribbon, she casually tied her ponytail with it and grinned at herself. She looked almost twelve again. Well, not quite. Her generous curves weren't hidden even under the bulky sweater and her hips were slender but rounded in the jeans.

She slipped on her wool socks and sneakers and then stretched. She was hungry and craved a cup of hot black coffee. How Lindsay had longed for this moment! All she wanted was to sit on the front step of the cabin and sip her coffee and enjoy the peace and serenity she hoped to find here.

Humming softly to herself, Lindsay headed for the kitchen, where she quickly made a breakfast of toast and coffee with hot scrambled eggs on a side plate. She wolfed down the food and ran outside with her mug of coffee.

Lindsay sat down and very quietly took in everything aound her, recalling pleasant memories of her childhood here with her father and mother and Jake. Her happiness was reflected in her face.

She soon realized that the light was becoming brighter and it occurred to her that she had slept later than she had thought. She smiled wryly. She hadn't looked at her watch once since she had come up here. It was a good sign. Lindsay had lived by time and clocks and schedules all her life, and now she could do as she pleased, whenever she pleased. Deciding to go for a walk, she put her coffee mug on the step.

Shortly after she started to stroll down the gravel road, she heard the sound of tires heading toward the cabin on the stony road. Quickly darting behind a tree, she glanced around. Lindsay laughed at herself when she realized that the car was the black Mercedes that Jason owned. She stepped from behind the tree and walked back toward the cabin.

Jason came to a stop and slowly stepped from the car, his eyes taking in the eager girl walking toward him. He grinned at her. She looked like a child with that beautiful hair tied up in a bouncy ponytail. She hadn't a speck of makeup on her face. She also looked a lot happier than the girl he had left last night. She had a devilish grin on her tiny face, almost an impishness about her. For a brief moment he was reminded of a time many many years ago when he had seen her with his father, always happy and eager to learn new things. His eyes squinted in the sun as she called his name. He had no idea of the impression he was making on Lindsay at this moment.

Lindsay had been thrilled to see him again so quickly. He had promised to check in on her but she was surprised to see he had meant to do so in such a short time.

When he stepped out of the car and stood there, with the sun streaming brightly over him, she immediately was reminded of how darkly and dangerously attractive he was. He was wearing a heavy navy blue flannel shirt, open at the neck, and tight-fitting jeans that once again defined the lean muscles of his hips and thighs. He leaned nonchalantly against the car door, watching her, his eyes never leaving her graceful body. He was wearing hiking boots and appeared even more good-looking than he had the night before. Her step faltered and she stopped momentarily to gain control of her senses. His black eyes were glittering, giving him a sensual appearance. Suddenly his face became unreadable, as if he were hiding some thought from her. She realized that he was scrutinizing her. His eyes slowly went over her body from the ponytail to her sneaker-clad feet, which she was now digging into the gravel uncertainly.

He truly looked like an Indian now. She wet her lips and proceeded toward him as he still watched her. When she was within four feet of him, he immediately put out a long arm and said, "Stop! Stop! Is this the same very tired and lonely girl that I almost tucked into bed last night? What happened to those circles under the eyes and the hopelessness in that beautiful face? You look like a child in that get-up, a very fetching child, I might add." He grinned suddenly, and her face lit up. He was making fun of her and she was enjoying it!

She laughed and said, "I was just going for a walk, Jason. I'm so glad it was you. I heard the tires and was afraid it was someone else."

"It couldn't be anyone else, Lindsay. Only my father or I ever come up here. His fishing cronies only come when he's here, and they all know he's away now. You don't know of anyone else who knows where this cabin is, do you?" His voice had become very soft, as if in warning.

She looked up at him and said, "No, Jason, I don't know of anyone who would ever think of coming to this cabin. I've never mentioned it to anyone. It was too private and held too many precious memories. I didn't want to share it with anyone."

"Not even Alec?" Jason asked, his question deceptively casual. Her eyes were clear as they looked up, candid and wide. He stared intently into them and felt a sudden flash of emotion shoot through him. If he wasn't careful, this girl was going to end up wrapping him around her little finger with those eyes, so childlike and innocent.

She was so unprotected and vulnerable, yet he knew she would be the last person in the world to admit it. She could be hurt so easily and he didn't want to be the one to hurt her. She seemed to trust him and he mustn't abuse that trust by frightening her. But damn, given five minutes with her, he couldn't control the instinctively strong feelings that surged through him—a combination of compassion and sensual attraction that overcame him.

He deliberately looked away from her and said casually, "I stopped by for two reasons. First, there's no phone in the cabin, as you have already surmised. I thought you might want to phone your father before it gets any later. He's probably waiting for a call. I'll drive you over to my home on Lake Raponda and you can use my phone, okay?"

Lindsay threw her arms around Jason's neck and hugged him. "Oh, thanks, Jason. I forgot about the phone and I did want to call him today before he worried too much. He'll be pleased that I'm safe up here, especially if he knows you're around in case of an emergency. He won't tell anyone where I am. I really appreciate your thoughtfulness."

Suddenly Lindsay became aware of the closeness of Jason's lean, hard body pressed against hers, and she pulled away. Her heart hammered as she swallowed and asked in a husky whisper, "How about a cup of coffee? It's still hot and I make a darn good pot, if I do say so myself." She looked up at his still countenance with an appeal in her eyes. He smiled in answer.

"Sounds good. Let me help you carry the tray outside. I know the perfect place near here. Perhaps I can show you some colorful scenery that might give you some ideas for your painting. As you remember, there are some mighty pretty woodlands around here, and I seem to remember a stream and a waterfall about four hundred yards away."

He smiled as she looked up at him eagerly. She ran into the cabin and soon emerged with a tray containing a pot of hot coffee, two mugs, and some sketch pads and pencils. She remembered that Jason rarely used cream or sugar.

He took the coffee from her and the two of them walked down the gravel road toward the wooded area in the back of the garage. The sun shone brightly as they chatted with ease.

"Jason, I do remember a waterfall somewhere around here. Jake took me there one day. Now I'll be able to find it quickly and start painting it. I want to get some of these scenes on canvas before the leaves come and go. If I get the basic sketches down on canvas, I can paint them later indoors. I'll remember the colors I don't finish, believe me." She stopped suddenly, aware that he was looking down at her with amusement.

"You love to paint, don't you, Lindsay?" His eyes glinted as she nodded eagerly. "Then we had better get going, young woman, for the frost will hit before you get those sketches down."

She turned and started down the road but he grabbed her arm, pulling her back for a brief moment. Looking down at her fragile, beautiful face, framed by the blue-black of her shiny hair, he asked, "Why didn't you ever pursue a career in painting, Lindsay? Surely it couldn't have been for the lack of wanting to or the lack of money. Your father would have been glad to help you. What kept you from doing what you really wanted to do?"

Lindsay frowned. "Jason, you're a man, one who has always done what he wanted to do. Perhaps the only man who could influence your thinking is your father. Well, I was sent away to Europe to learn the graces, the ways of pleasing men, and when I returned home, the most important man in my life was my father, whom I loved a great deal. He sent me away to become polished and cultured, and I returned home with my heart set on only one thing—to be everything he ever expected of me. Now I think all he ever really wanted was me to be happy. But I wasn't trained to work in the usual sense. I mean, how many jobs require a degree in French cooking or knowing what silver to serve with what place setting? I was so busy making out menus and planning seating arrangements that I had little time for other hobbies."

She stopped for a brief moment, as if reorganizing her thoughts and then continued. "I had little time to go out during the day and not much time off to really concentrate on my painting. You see, Jason, you have to be able to spend the time and concentrate on a subject when you want to paint it. You have to have a subject that you love very much."

"And you never found either, the time or the subject, Lindsay?"

"No, I never found either. Can we drop it now, Jason? I really want to get to the stream and don't want to think about my other life anymore. I'm here now and that's what's really important. I want to paint and I have the opportunity, with your help, kind sir!" She laughed.

With one dark eyebrow raised, he murmured quietly, "I'll remember that, young lady. Some day you'll pay the piper. I'm not always so generous!" He glanced around him and placed the tray on the ground as they sat down, surrounded by brightly colored bushes and clump birch. Lindsay poured the coffee and they both sat in silence, enjoying the peaceful sounds of nature that surrounded them. Lindsay nodded to herself and seemed absorbed by her environment. She shyly glanced at Jason from under veiled lashes. He had rested his back against a tree and seemed remote, in a world of his own. She remembered the way Jake had described him in letters to her when she lived in Europe. She could almost imagine Jake in her place. Many times he and Jason had gone walking in the woods together when Jake had planned on painting a particular scene.

The two men had never talked much, but they understood each other and appreciated each other's feelings about the world of nature surrounding them. Each contemplated and enjoyed it in different ways. Jake loved to talk about the colors and textures around him, while Jason loved to sit and listen and watch quietly.

Lindsay watched Jason as she sipped her coffee. He

seemed to hear every sound made by the animals playing or scurrying past. He heard the words whispered between the streams and the trees and sky. He was a part of this world and seemed to find a peace here that most men can never hope to find in the world outside, with its noise and frenetic everyday life.

Lindsay felt that she was learning a little more about Jason and she hoped as time went on that she would get him to reveal even more, until he had unraveled the mystery that was Jason Mainwaring. Somehow he had learned the secret of coping and becoming financially secure in a modern, civilized world. At the same time he had been able to maintain his own identity. Perhaps he could help her do the same.

She still didn't understand why it was so important to her to know everything about this man, but right now it was enough to say that she could never abide an unsolved mystery, and Jason was still a mystery to her.

Perhaps an hour or two had quietly passed as Lindsay quickly sketched the scenes around her. Using her brightly colored chalk pencils, she rapidly recreated the landscape on page after page of her sketch pad. She was totally absorbed in her creations. Jason lay back, watching her, sipping coffee and occasionally breaking her concentration to draw her attention to the curious woodland animals that sat hidden behind bushes, busily chattering and watching the pair. Lindsay had never felt so relaxed and happy in her life. She shivered and felt warm hands give her shoulders a gentle shake. Startled, she turned to see Jason reaching down to help her up.

"It's getting chilly. We best get back to the cabin. If you didn't have someone to watch over you, young lady, I believe you'd spend the rest of the day here and catch pneumonia!"

She laughed and gathered up her materials as Jason carried the tray with the empty coffee mugs. Carefully they made their way back to the gravel road.

As Lindsay carried the tray into the kitchen to make

some more coffee and sandwiches, Jason started a fire in the living room.

"After we eat, could we go over to your house, Jason, so I can phone Father?" Lindsay asked as she carried the sandwiches over to the coffee table and sat down.

"Fine, but first I want to take a look at those sketches, and don't pull the temperamental artist bit on me. I deserve to see them, especially after I showed you where the waterfall was and sat on that damn ground for two hours without making a sound!" His eyes crinkled, yet Lindsay was certain his set lips would brook no defiance. She bit her lip, afraid he would think her sketches the work of a bungling amateur. Most of all, she knew that secretly she was afraid Jason wouldn't approve of them. Raising her chin pugnaciously in the air, she decided to refuse to be intimidated by him. If he didn't like them, too bad!

She tossed the pad into his lap and stood there, hands on her hips, ready to do battle if necessary. Jason set his cup of coffee down and studied each quick sketch, his face immobile, unreadable. His expression didn't change and when he had finished, he sat staring down at the sketch pad on his lap. Finally, when she thought she could stand it no longer, he looked up at her and studied her apprehensive face.

"I don't know that much about what makes an artist good, but unless my eyes are deceiving me, these sketches are damn good. You've managed to capture the true colors and total composition of nature with just a few lines. You do have talent, Lindsay, and my father would be the first to admit it. Why the hell did you waste all those years?" He shook his head and Lindsay stood shaking like a leaf, afraid to destroy the feeling of the moment with a few words. Tears glistened in her eyes and her full lips quivered as she tried to smile her thanks to Jason. He seemed to realize the importance his statement held for her and pulled her down to the sofa, cradling her soft head on his hard shoulder.

"Hey, what's this? I give you a completely unprofessional opinion, and you go soft on me. I'm hardly an expert you know, so stop it!"

Lindsay looked down at the strong hands covering her tiny ones and suddenly felt the tears that had so long been held back force themselves to her lashes. Swallowing quickly, she shook her head, murmuring, "I'm sorry, Jason, I don't make it a habit to cry, believe me. I think the last time I cried was when my mother died in that accident when I was twelve. I don't know what came over me. I just never had anyone compliment me on something that meant so much to me. Even when I was in school in Europe all those years, without father near me, I excelled in painting, but no one really took it seriously." Her voice lowered. "It was lonely, Jason, without Father or Jake. I mean, I was well cared for, but something was missing."

"Love, Lindsay, that was what was missing. You were dutifully cared for, but not loved . . . not loved."

She looked up at him again amazed at his perception.

"It is important, Jason, especially when you're growing up alone," she whispered huskily.

Jason nodded, reminded of the great affection he and his father had always shared and still did. Lindsay bit her bottom lip, fighting to keep back the tears that again threatened to overcome her, tears for the love lost between Alec and herself and for something else that Lindsay couldn't quite name, something that was just beyond reach, something that had to do with the dark, understanding stranger sitting calmly next to her with an arm held protectively around her shoulders.

Jason smiled at Lindsay. As fragile as she appeared on the outside, it would seem she was determined to overcome any sign of weakness like a few tears, and yet, Jason thought, what other woman did he know who, placed under the same circumstances as Lindsay, would have reacted to them as realistically as she had? Denied love while growing up, she had made the best of it. Wanting to cry, she had stopped herself. She was indeed her father's daughter. Jason smiled to himself as he thought of the next few weeks and what they would have in store for this beautiful, troubled girl. Watching her, he understood her feelings. He disdained the press as much as Lindsay. The reporters would be frantic, wondering where she had gone. Knowing Ray Sheffield like he did, Jason also knew that the old man would enjoy discouraging the press. He chuckled and looked down at Lindsay as she sipped the coffee he handed her.

"What's so funny, Jason? I'm sure that calming tearful women is not exactly your forte," she murmured drily.

"I was just imagining the tabloids in the next few days. I hope your poor Alec has the sense to disappear for a while. You've really provided them with enough speculation to write the front pages of the gossip columns for another two weeks! I hope your father is up to it, the old devil."

She laughed as Jason stood up. "He'll manage beautifully! In fact, he'll enjoy every moment of it. Now that I look back on it, I think something was bothering him about Alec and me. He looked worried before I went to Bermuda. I think he guessed how I felt long before I did.

"Jason, I don't want to dwell on what was. You know enough about me by now. I've practically given you my life history from the time I was a skinny child until now. Now it's your turn. Tell me about these homes you build that Jake is so proud of. I understand from him that you travel worldwide to complete them, and yet you always return home here. What's it like, Jason, to really create something that you love, from the ground up?"

Jason placed another log on the fire, then sat down opposite her on a comfortable chair. Lindsay looked at him and once again felt her heart begin to pound violently. A warmth invaded the pit of her stomach, spreading down to weaken her knees. Jason's very presence exuded a primitive sexuality, and she was becoming more and more susceptible to it.

Jason leaned back in the chair and studied his long legs stretched out before him. "Ah yes, my houses. Yes, I do design houses, but to me they're special houses, Lindsay. I can't stand the modern concrete slabs that are put up one by one, all in a row, each one a different color so you can tell which one you live in. There are no trees, of course, because the first thing the contractor does is tear out every living thing in order to move in his large machinery. It destroys the wildlife as well as the greenery. Trees take hundreds of years to grow and only a few moments of man's carelessness and uncaring to tear them down."

Lindsay watched Jason's dark face, turned almost savage in his anger as it reflected the flickering flames from the fireplace.

Jason continued after a brief moment. "I chose to combine the best of two worlds; my love of the outdoors and my love of designing buildings. I built around natural elements to create houses that fit into the land without forcing the land to mold itself around a house.

"Needless to say, in the beginning my ideas were a bit unorthodox and it cost a great deal of money to build a house and keep the landscape intact. But gradually more and more calls from all over the world came in, and of course more requests for distinctive designs."

Lindsay sat enraptured at the quiet spell Jason was weaving over her as he spoke of his work. She was seeing a side of this man she was certain many had not, and for some unknown reason, she was happy and content just to sit and listen to his voice.

"I try to work mainly with the natural elements, like redwood and stone and glass, so the buyer can look out from every room and enjoy the land that he has purchased."

Lindsay could see the softening in Jason's face as it creased in slight pride and pleasure as he thought of his creations. He looked up at her and continued as he noted her absorption in his words. "It's a challenge and in the end it gives me the deepest pleasure and contentment to see a beautiful piece of scenery untouched, and yet, to have someone living in a home I have created for them and enjoying it as much as I did designing and building it. One can look out any large window and see different scenery—trees of many colors and shapes, an ocean breaking on huge boulders, sand dunes with palm trees waving, tropical underbrush. Everything that was there in the beginning, untouched as they first saw it."

He sighed softly. "But in the end, when the building is completed and the work is over, I have had it with mankind in general—the red tape, the obligatory parties and social functions, the necessary meetings with heads of state. Then I have to get away and return to my Vermont woods and the peace that I know I shall find here." He stopped talking and gazed into the fire.

Lindsay whispered softly, "And you came back this time to get away and found me here to interrupt your peace and quiet. I'm so sorry, Jason. Maybe I should leave after all."

Jason looked at her swiftly, his voice suddenly harsh and arrogant. "You'll do no such thing! You're here to stay, Lindsay, and don't you forget it! You're no bother to me at all. I have my own design studio at the house and it's quite comfortable. I only stopped by here, don't forget, to check the cabin. You're not leaving, do you understand?" His eyes glared and his jaw was set.

Nodding slowly, Lindsay realized that this was a Jason she hadn't met before. He was now the world-famous architect, demanding something and expecting immediate obedience. For some reason, deep in her heart, she was glad he felt so strongly that she stay.

"And now, I think I had better drive you over to my home. You have to phone your father, and I want to look over my mail. Are you ready?" He stood up and reached for a windbreaker on a hook on the wall and handed it to Lindsay. She took it and looked around the cabin.

"Forget the dishes," he said. "You can do them later. I don't think we should wait anymore to phone Ray. He'll be worried if he doesn't hear from you by this afternoon, and I want him to know you're safe with me."

Lindsay felt mischievous and asked sweetly, "And am I safe with you, Jason?" She gazed at him from under seductive, long lashes and her lips quivered with laughter.

"Don't play the siren with me, young lady, or you'll rue

'm a hell of a lot more experienced you don't stop playing Lola with me, you hadn't started this!" His eyes ...ay immediately regretted her words, ...son would not hesitate to follow through ...ng if further provoked. She looked down de- ...t her feet and answered quietly, "Yes, Jason. ...ever you say . . ." Under her breath she finished the ...ntence, "You big bully." Unfortunately for her, Jason heard and grabbed her forcefully by the shoulders, looking down at her widened eyes.

"Why is it that you like to provoke me? If it's a lesson you need, then, by God, it's a lesson you'll get!" And with that he pulled her pliant body to his own hardness, molding her against him as one hand arched her against his hips and the other swung up behind her neck and under her head to press her shocked lips to his own. Her open-mouthed protest was smothered as his firm lips covered her full ones and gently worked their magic until he obtained the response that he demanded. As Lindsay felt herself melt against his hard, demanding body, she became aware of an intense heat invading her own, forcing her own responsive body to arch instinctively against Jason's. Her head pounded loudly and there was a loud ringing in her ears. She felt as if she were drowning in his kiss, and her arms wrapped around his neck to prevent her legs from giving out. The room swirled around her and she longed to stay in Jason's arms forever. She had never felt like this before and if there had ever been a time to deny the fact that she and Jason were attracted to each other in a purely sexual way, it was too late now. She could not deny the primitive feelings Jason aroused in her. To him it was just another game, but to her it was a deeply personal emotion, one that only he had ever awakened.

Just when she thought she would die if Jason didn't stop his assault, he immediately broke off, and glared down at her. Taking a ragged breath, he warned, "I'm telling you now, Lindsay. I'm a man and you can push me just so far!

Try teasing me the next time and I won't be resp
for how far I go! Do you understand?"

Numbly, she nodded. She wasn't even certain she c
have answered him. Her senses were devastated. She
still shaking.

Taking her by the arm, Jason led her roughly down the
steps and opened the car door. He dumped her unceremoniously into the front seat and slammed the door. She
forced herself to stare straight ahead. He got in the car
and backed out of the gravel driveway, straightening the
wheels and continued on down the Molly Trail toward his
home on Lake Raponda. Lindsay allowed herself a sideways glance at him. His jaw was set and his eyes were set
straight ahead on the road. She noted that a muscle in his
neck occasionally ticked uncontrollably and his long, tense
fingers held the steering wheel tightly. She realized then
that the kiss had disturbed him as greatly as she knew it
had disturbed her. With a slight smile she settled back in
the cozy comfort of the bucket seat and gazed out at the
beautiful countryside.

Chapter Seven

Jason pulled into the stone drive to his house. The lights were on and he frowned, his eyes squinting in a scowl. He cursed softly as he recognized a car parked in the driveway. Lindsay glanced around but could see no one, and wondered why Jason seemed so upset.

He shook his head and straightened his back as he slowly got out of the car. He stood there a moment, staring at the lighted window, his lips taut. With a quick glance at Lindsay, he motioned to her to follow him. They walked silently to the house, Lindsay afraid to speak.

Jason unlocked the door, opened it quietly, and walked into the wide, marble-floored hallway. He stopped suddenly and Lindsay bumped into him. He motioned for her to stay where she was and then walked to the living room doorway.

Lindsay's view was blocked by his broad back. Frowning with curiosity, she moved to the side of the doorway and peeked into the large, bright room. It had been decorated in white and cool blue and accented with several large hanging baskets of deep green plants. The wide window allowed the bright sun to add to the impression of airy roominess. Lindsay was certain that Jason had designed this room.

A slight movement from a long sofa placed against a

wall drew Lindsay's attention. Now she knew the reason for Jason's sudden stiffness. A tiny figure in gold and cream was draped along the sofa, reclining with a drink in one perfectly manicured hand, and a cigarette in the other, casually exhaling smoke. Her artfully made-up face was a study of composed sophistication.

Jason stood looking at her from the doorway, his face inscrutable. The woman turned her head slowly and her eyes widened, as if just realizing that he was there. Lindsay watched with amazement as Jason smiled to himself. He obviously knew this woman very well.

Lindsay felt an instinctive chill. She bit her bottom lip and stepped back until Jason called to her. For some reason she felt frightened and wondered why this woman felt so at home in Jason's home. Her heart beat harder as she wondered exactly what kind of relationship this cold-looking woman had with Jason.

She must have heard his car in the stone drive, yet she managed to present a picture of casual stylishness. Lindsay thought drily that all she needed was a box of chocolate candy on the table next to her and the picture would be complete. Strange, her immediate dislike for this stranger. It wasn't like her at all.

The pale blonde looked up and, smiling knowingly to herself, whispered huskily, "Hello, darling, I've been waiting for you. What took you so long?"

A frown appeared on Jason's inscrutable face. Lindsay had the distinct impression that no one ever questioned him. This woman must have known it, because she immediately backed off and smiled at him.

He looked back at her and Lindsay heard his whisper tightly, "Leave it, Marcia!" So her name was Marcia. Lindsay felt a lump gather in her throat as she realized that this woman and Jason Mainwaring were not just friends. Somehow the thought made her uneasy. She longed to leave the hallway, anything to get away from this woman's cloying presence.

Marcia's carefully penciled eyes widened and an eyebrow arched at Jason's tone. Apparently he had never spoken to her like this. From Marcia's expression, Lindsay could tell that she was curious about what had put him in such ill humor.

Marcia smiled brightly and slid off the sofa. She walked gracefully over to the bar and poured a drink, and then approached Jason, her head cocked seductively to one side, and handed the glass to him. He took it from her and sat it down on a side table. Marcia placed her arms possessively around his neck and said with a pout, "Don't be angry with me, darling, for coming in when you weren't here. I just wanted to surprise you. Aren't you glad to see me, Jason?"

Lindsay felt stifled by the scene she was witnessing and longed to leave. But Jason had promised she could use his phone to call her father and she had to phone him that day. All she could do was wait. What was Jason waiting for, damn him! Why didn't he just tell Marcia that there was someone else in the house with them. She didn't appreciate being exposed to their sickening lovemaking. How could Jason do this to her?

Jason looked into Marcia's wide blue eyes and firmly disengaged her arms, shaking his head. "Not now, Marcia. I'm not in the mood." His expression was coolly remote.

Lindsay saw Marcia's face turn icy as her anger surfaced. "That's obvious, Jason, but would you mind telling me what's wrong with you? Are you ill? You've never acted like this before!"

Jason frowned, his back to her, and finished the drink he had picked up from the table. He turned slightly and nodded. "Yes, I have a lot of work to catch up on since I've been away. I've loads of mail to go through, and I think I'll probably be up all night if I'm going to wade through the damn pile. And there is something else, Marcia. I'd like you to meet someone. Perhaps you've heard my father speak of her. My cousin Lindsay is here for a vacation. She's staying in the cabin for a while. I brought her over to use the phone upstairs. I think I hear her coming down the stairs now. Yes, here she comes."

Lindsay almost choked in anger as she heard Jason

casually call her. He had deliberately made Marcia think she was upstairs all the time. Why? To save Marcia embarrassment? Lindsay couldn't imagine that cold blonde feeling embarrassment over anything.

She straightened her shoulders and entered the room, glaring daggers at Jason. He seemed amused and walked over to her and casually placed a brotherly arm around her shoulders, pressing them as if in warning. She held her tongue and forced a smile to her tight lips.

Marcia's sharp eyes took in Lindsay, looked at Jason and asked sharply, "Your cousin, you say? Funny, I don't think I ever heard you mention her before, Jason. She's a bit young to be staying at the cabin alone, don't you think? Where are her parents?"

Jason answered blandly, "I've been asked to watch over this child, to make sure she doesn't get into any trouble. She's usually pretty well-behaved if she isn't left to her own devices. Isn't that right, cousin?" Black sparks of amusement flew from his eyes into her now raging ones. Lindsay knew she looked younger than she really was but Jason was taking full advantage of the fact—at her expense. She remembered the last time she had thwarted him and the devastating consequences he had imposed upon her. Her lips still tingled from that assault.

Her thoughts were abruptly brought back to the present when she looked over at Marcia, who gave her a brilliant, welcoming smile and held out her tiny hand. "Well, I hope you won't take Jason away from his work too often, Linda. He's a very important man and tries to limit his social life when he's working here at the house. If there is anything you need or want, please feel free to call me. I have so much more time than Jason and I'm sure you would rather have another woman to talk with. Perhaps I can take you shopping into Bennington. All girls your age love new wardrobes, don't they?"

Lindsay felt Jason tighten his hold on her shoulder and pull her against him warningly. She couldn't have moved if she had wanted to. She was certain he could feel the trembling rage within her at being patronized by this cold woman.

She looked at Marcia and forced herself to answer sweetly, "The name is Lindsay, not Linda, and thank you for your kind offer, but believe me, Jason has done more than enough for me already! In fact, I just can't think of how I can thank him sufficiently for all he has done today! His help has been totally unexpected, and I can only look forward to the day when I can repay him fully!" She looked up at Jason with stormy eyes, and caught the quirk of amusement at the corner of his firm lips. Her underlying threat had not gone unnoticed.

She turned to Marcia and caught a brittle smile forcing its way through tight lips. The smile did not reach the cold blue eyes, and Lindsay realized that she had made a bitter enemy of this woman and for only one reason—Marcia was hatefully jealous of Lindsay.

Lindsay caught her breath and looked away as Marcia shrugged and smiled coolly. Walking gracefully over to Jason, she deliberately drew his arm away from Lindsay and pulled him toward the doorway, not giving Lindsay a second glance. "Darling, you do look tired and I shouldn't have come over to bother you like this. You go ahead with your work and I'll see you later. Why don't I drive your cousin back to the cabin and save you some time?"

Jason shook his head and smiled. "Thanks, Marcia, but I want to make certain the cabin's okay. I don't want you driving over there alone either. Now out! I'm busy and I have to make some phone calls!"

Seemingly satisfied with his answer, Marcia gazed up at him and ran a hand through his thick hair. He glanced down at her short silvery blond hair and her tiny figure. Lindsay was certain that Marcia was fully aware of how her curves were accentuated by the clinging silk dress. She sighed to herself as Marcia placed her hands around Jason's waist as he bent down and briefly kissed her, then turned her toward the door. As she swept out the door, she turned and blew him a kiss.

"I'll see you tomorrow then, darling. You did promise to take Daddy fishing tomorrow."

Jason stood in the doorway and watched her drive away, her sharply turned wheels throwing stones. He stared after her for a long time, long after she had disappeared.

Lindsay stood in the hallway, her hands on both hips in a stance of defiance. She was shaking with anger. "You beast! I don't give a damn what you do in your spare time, but how dare you expose me to that cute welcome-home scene between you and your girlfriend! I've never been so embarrassed in my life, standing outside the room like an eavesdropper. Why didn't you send me upstairs to use the phone like you told Marcia? She's really sweet, that one. If she could have, she would have nailed me to the wall with the daggers she was shooting at me from those glacial eyes. And don't give me that look, Jason Mainwaring. I'm not used to having complete strangers look me over like I'm some sort of distasteful creature that just happened to invade her happy little world! The way she acted, you'd think she thought we were having a mad, passionate love affair behind her back." She glared at Jason's impassive face and couldn't resist adding, "Possessive, isn't she, Jason? And I thought you were impervious to dominating females!"

Jason's dark eyes glinted as he ran them over her taut figure, hovering momentarily on her slender breasts and hips. "Why, I do believe there are deeper and more primitive depths to you than one would expect from the well-bred daughter of one of the more socially prominent families! Lindsay, my dear, your claws are showing." He started to chuckle, then closed the door, turning to face Lindsay completely.

"Don't you laugh at me, Jason! I have no intention of getting involved in your private life, and I definitely don't appreciate you telling your girlfriend that you're here to watch over me. I'm quite capable of taking care of myself, thank you. I was doing quite well before you came barging into the cabin. All I want to do is to borrow your phone so I can call my father." She raised her chin with dignity. "If you'll tell me where the phone is, I'll leave you to your time-consuming work. Heaven knows, I wouldn't want to bother you!"

Lindsay turned abruptly to the stairs, placed a hand on the finely polished wood railing, and waited for him to join her, her lips held in a tight line of defiance. Jason stood staring at her, his dark face intent, and then folded well-muscled arms across his chest, taking in her mutinous look.

"Are you certain you really want me to escort you upstairs to the phone? It might be in a bedroom, and the temptation of being alone upstairs with you when you're beautiful and angry might be my undoing. But then you did ask me, didn't you, and so, being a gentleman and host, I had better show you where the phone is after all!" His eyes seemed to twinkle and Lindsay eyed him warily, not sure whether or not he was serious. His lips quirked with a slight smile of amusement, yet his black eyes flashed something else, some sort of a message. Again she was aware of his virility, dark and frightening, and of something unknown that was awakening warm and deep sensations in her, warning her of possible dangers of hidden pleasures and delights.

"Jason, don't be silly! Stop teasing me. You heard what Marcia said. She thinks I'm a teenager and I most certainly look like one right now. You said so yourself. She'd be furious if she knew my real age and who I was!"

Jason nodded his dark head in agreement. "And now perhaps you'll stop jumping to conclusions. That's exactly why I didn't want Marcia to catch you walking in with me. She's as sharp as a tack. Don't let her fragile appearance fool you for one minute. She'd have hit you with so many questions that you'd have panicked. It was better that I paved the way. I can handle Marcia. We understand each other very well. Believe me, Lindsay, she's a tigress when she wants something, and I appreciate that facet of her personality. I understand it because I go after something I want, too. It might also interest you to know that her father runs the local paper and Marcia handles all the social events in the local areas and in the larger towns like New York and Washington. It wouldn't have taken her long to put two and two together and figure out who you were. Even I couldn't stop her from printing the fact that you were up here. She'd have photographers camping on your doorstep!"

"Jason, you appear to be—well, more than friends. Would she still do that if you told her not to? She must know how much you dislike to have your own privacy invaded. Wouldn't she do the same for me, especially if you requested it of her?"

Jason frowned and threw his arm out in the air. "Lindsay, despite what you think, you can't hide the fact that you are a beautiful girl. And the very fact that I have taken you under my wing, as Marcia believes, would be enough to make any woman suspicious. How long do you think you'll be able to hide the fact that you're quite an attractive and desirable woman? You'll just have to maintain a low profile for a while, and she'll eventually forget about you."

Lindsay looked at Jason's intent face and realized that he was right. But she also understood something else that he was totally unaware of—that Marcia hated her as she would have hated any woman Jason was involved with, no matter how innocent the circumstances. She was also still recovering from the compliment that he had paid her, perhaps without thinking. He saw her as desirable and attractive, and the very fact that he thought that made her wary of her own traitorous emotions.

Bending her head in slight defeat, she nodded to him. She would do as he asked, even though it galled her to think she had to hide her activities from Marcia like some criminal.

"Ready to see the house now?" His quiet voice interrupted her thoughts. She forced a smile to her lips and took a step toward the spiral staircase.

"Jason, I'm sorry if I'm going to be the cause of any trouble between you and Marcia," she said. "It's none of my business and I had no right to make such bitchy remarks about her like I did. I can't imagine why I resented her attitude toward me so much. I hope you won't change your opinion of me too much after that."

She looked at him hopefully. He gazed solemnly at her, and answered after a moment. "Oh, believe me, Lindsay, nothing will make me change the way I feel about you. Once I form an opinion I rarely change it, not even when you act impulsively or like a little spitfire. All you need is a little redirecting and, since I'm here, I might as well take on the job!" He laughed at the outraged look on her face.

Lindsay stamped her foot and pointed a shaking finger in his face. "You are the most insufferable man it has ever been my misfortune to meet! I take back everything I said before about watching myself. You and your friend Marcia are two of a kind! You're arrogant and hard-nosed and stubborn and snobs! Now show me that phone!"

She started up the winding staircase and heard his soft steps following her. As she reached the top, she came to a dead stop.

Instead of finding a hallway on the second floor of the house as she had expected, she found herself gazing into one room taking up the entire second story. Her hand gripped the spiral railing as she gazed spellbound into the enormous room. It was designed as a world unto itself. As she felt a gentle push from Jason, she stepped forward into the room, shaking her head in disbelief. She murmured softly, "Oh, Jason, it's beautiful. And so unexpected! I thought the bedrooms would be up here." Jason walked around Lindsay and took in the bemused look on her face.

"Do you approve of my design, Lindsay?" Jason asked quietly, with an intensity in his soft voice that she had not noticed before. She found herself unable to speak and could only nod.

Jason looked around the room and took her by the elbow. "Here, I'll show you around. I designed this house and built it to suit only one person—me. This entire floor is based on the concept that one needs room to breathe, and yet at the same time should be able to entertain a group of friends without everyone feeling closed in. As you can see, two-thirds of the room is actually a large living room. I've placed the sofas and chairs around the room in a large rectangle so that each of the walls can be viewed from any angle. Except there aren't really any walls. I decided to surround the entire three walls with Thermaglas panes. That way I can look out above the trees and see the mountains any time of the year. It's particularly effective right now with the fall colors."

Lindsay nodded, thinking that it was like living in a large tree house of your own. No painting could have come close to capturing the natural beauty of the countryside that one could view from any vantage point in the living room. The room was truly the work of an inspired artist.

Her eyes took in the low, circular stone fireplace in the center of the room. Surrounding it lay an assortment of comfortable, large, colored pillows that invited one to plop down and enjoy the view. She imagined the crisp cold of coming winter the glowing embers of a fire sending their warmth across the room. She smiled at the thought.

"What are you thinking, Lindsay? There's a bit of a devil in that smile!"

"I was just imagining what a perfect scene for seduction, with that view and a cozy fire and all those pillows! But of course, that never entered your mind when you designed it, did it, Jason?" She grinned up at him as he raised his dark brows in mock censure.

"Lindsay! You don't trust me at all! I designed this room with only one thing in mind—to make my friends comfortable in pleasant surroundings. But now that you mention it . . ."

Lindsay laughed and moved further into the room. Suddenly she stopped right in her tracks, her mouth dropping open in surprise.

At the farthest end of the room, exposed to the rest of the large living room, Jason had built an open kitchen, with a sink and range, plus a center working area. They faced the large room so that whoever was cooking could still participate in the general conversation in the room. There were no walls in Jason's house to isolate the person in the kitchen area from the people in the rest of the room. The arrangement lent an air of spaciousness and congeniality.

The fourth wall of the room was the kitchen wall, composed entirely of old brick and covered with useful cupboards. The only dividing line between the kitchen area and the large living area was a long butcher-block counter with high-backed chairs pushed under the counter from the living room side.

"I take it you approve, Lindsay? Any suggestions from the girl who was educated in the fine arts of cooking in Europe? It isn't quite finished yet and I left it 'til last because I don't do that much cooking for myself."

She ran her fingers across the counter and walked into the kitchen area, opening the cupboards and testing the stove. "It's designed with such efficiency and logic, as well as beauty," she said. "I've never seen such a productive home kitchen in my life. Why, any woman would give her right arm just to cook one dinner here! Why, with the few necessary cooking tools—like whisks and wooden spoons and a few cooper bowls and worthwhile pans—it would be perfect!"

"Where would you put all those things without cluttering up the counter, though?" Jason questioned casually.

"Why, you'd hang wrought iron circular pan and tool holders over the sink and stove area, suspended from the ceiling! That way they would be out of the way, yet handy to reach when you needed them! Just like a French kitchen, Jason. Oh, this is the most unusual living room I've ever seen. You really should be proud of yourself. Your friends must love coming here."

"No one's ever been here, except Marcia, and she isn't interested in kitchens. She prefers to stay in the study when she visits. It's more civilized. So actually, you're the first person I've ever given the tour to. And you haven't even seen the complete house. Interested in continuing?" he asked.

Lindsay swallowed as she felt her heart beat more quickly. Why had Jason never shown his house to anyone else? He had said very little when she had made her comments, yet she had the distinct impression that he was very interested in them. She frowned and wrinkled her nose. Jason was certainly behaving strangely. A sudden thought came to her—the bedrooms! Where were the bedrooms she had expected to find when she'had come upstairs? Certainly the circular staircase had surprised her, but now she could see its purpose.

"Jason, where are the bedrooms? I thought you said they were up here."

He raised his dark brows and his eyes glinted dangerously as he answered, "Did I? Funny, but I remember you were the one to insist that you come upstairs to make your phone call."

"All right, all right, I'll admit for once that you're right, but that still doesn't explain where you put the bedrooms."

He laughed at her discomfort and pointed to an area behind the kitchen. Lindsay squinted and noted that a narrow path led beyond the kitchen wall. She looked questioningly at Jason.

"The house is built like a large 'L,' " he explained. "As you enter the front of the house, it looks like a large rectangle, but actually when you reach the end of the rectangle, the house swings to the left, into another rectangle, or the bottom of the 'L.' Here, you'll understand in a minute."

He walked quickly ahead of her and swung open what appeared to be a large bar door beyond the kitchen wall. Behind the brick wall Lindsay saw a compact but brilliantly colored powder room for guests. Directly in front of them was a heavy pecan wood door, shining in a satin glow. He leaned in front of Lindsay and pushed the heavy door open and stepped aside.

Lindsay gave him a quick glance and stepped into the room. It was obviously a very large master bedroom that took up the entire back of the house, or the remainder of the 'L' shape that Jason had described earlier. It was also a very masculine room, stark in its simplicity, yet with its blend of woodland colors—deep brown shag rugs, soft beige walls, and creamy yellow velvet chairs—it gave an immediate impression of a peaceful haven. Lindsay noticed a small writing desk in ivory tones against one wall, and wide, paneled windows on each long wall. Her gaze fell on the enormous bed that seemed to take up an entire wall. She suddenly felt nervous as she glanced quickly at Jason. He noted her wary look with amusement and nodded.

"Yes, this is my room and I sleep in that bed. Comfortable looking, isn't it, kitten?" He seemed to be laughing at her, and she lifted her chin and glared at him, bright green lights coming from her eyes.

She defended herself sarcastically. "Well, it does seem exceptionally large, even in this room." She dared him to answer and, when he did, she suddenly had the impression she had started something she was in no position to finish gracefully!

"Well, let's just say I decided that when I sleep there are times when I want a lot of room. But then, on the other hand, it all depends on the time and the moment and believe me, little one, there are most definitely times when I wish that bed were not quite so large. Like right now, for instance."

Lindsay quickly stepped back and away from Jason as he started for her. "Jason, don't you dare! I most certainly did not offer any invitation to test the softness of your bed! You stay right there, do you hear me?" In near panic, she ran over to the desk and sat down in the stiff-backed chair, her heart pounding violently as she berated herself for once again giving Jason the advantage. He sat down on the bed and roared with laughter. She longed to pick up some object and throw it at him. She knew she was too vulnerable in this bedroom with Jason so near. Certainly it was only a game with him, but Lindsay was becoming increasingly aware that each time she and Jason confronted each other physically, she lost another battle.

With an urge as old as time itself, she lashed out in defense of her traitorous weakness.

"What does Marcia think of your color scheme, Jason? Since she isn't interested in cooking or the kitchen, I'm certain from the tiny bit I saw downstairs earlier, she must have an opinion of this room!"

Suddenly Jason's face darkened, and his eyes cooled as he gazed at Lindsay sitting straight in the chair. He stood up slowly and started for the door. He turned and said evenly, "If you've seen everything that could interest you in this room, we can leave now. I won't bother showing you the master bath. You might be afraid I'd want to take a shower with you. Let's go!"

He turned and stalked out of the room. Lindsay hesitantly followed him, feeling guilty and miserable. Why did she always ruin everything? He had only wanted to show her his domain. He was proud of it, and Jason was not a man to share his private feelings with many people. Why had she brought Marcia into it? She shook her head in disgust. By the time she reached the lower level, Jason was in his study, leafing through a large pile of mail.

She walked over and stood quietly next to him. "Jason, why do you sit there so calmly? Go ahead and let me have it. I deserve it. I had no right to make those snide remarks. I'm sure I have no right whatsoever to make any judgment on any of your friends, and you certainly owe me one kick in the butt after my unforgivable behavior. Your home is lovely. I sincerely mean it, and if there was any way I could make up for my rudeness, I'd do it in a minute! Please, Jason. Look at me?"

Her eyes appealed to him as he turned his head slightly and stopped leafing through the mail. He stared intently at her for a long time and finally nodded briefly. With a deep sigh he pursed his slim lips together and said slowly, "I'm not a patient man, Lindsay. I have never been one and, quite frankly, I've never answered to anyone but myself. Before you entered my life last night, I led a reasonably peaceful existence, and I'm certain you don't deliberately mean to do the little things that you unwittingly do to cause my well-fortified walls of security and peace to come crumbling down around me. So let's start over. Right now. You want to make amends? Fine. I'll hold you to that promise. No more remarks about Marcia. Is that understood?"

Lindsay hung her head and tried not to grimace in disgust as she nodded her head. Her black hair hung around her face, making her look like a child caught with her hand in the cookie jar. Her ponytail had come undone long ago, and she had stuffed the ribbon into the pocket of her jeans. Despite what Jason felt for Marcia, Lindsay still rebelliously felt deep down that the woman was a selfish, spoiled bitch who was out to snatch Jason. How could he be so stupid?

"All right, now let's continue the tour, and then you can call your father. Then I think I'll take you out to get some lunch. I'm getting hungry myself, and knowing your appetite as I do, you won't refuse the invitation!" He smiled and reached a long finger out to raise up her chin. His eyes danced as he took in the repentant look she gave him. Standing up, he took her by the hand and led her out of the study and on down the hall.

As they walked toward the back of the house, Jason pointed out three other bedrooms, each with its own bath. These three bedrooms and Jason's study took up the bottom floor. When they reached the back, she realized that the master bedroom was situated directly overhead. Once again there was a small powder room located on the lower floor, directly under the one upstairs.

Jason opened a door and Lindsay found herself walking into a large den, complete with a balcony that overlooked the back of the house. As she walked through it, she came to a sectioned-off area that she recognized as a well-organized laundry room, complete with washer, dryer, and an extra-large freezer. Jason explained that this was what was called a "mud room" in New England.

"If the kids come into the house in bad weather, they always come in through the 'mud room.' I designed the den so that the kids will have their own large area to play

105

in when the weather is very bad outside. It's away from the upstairs, as are the bedrooms."

Lindsay felt a lump fill her throat and forced herself to ask, "What kids, Jason? I haven't seen any here. Do the neighborhood kids come here to play? I don't understand. Why do you have so many bedrooms?"

He looked down at her and answered matter-of-factly, "Why, my kids, Lindsay. I'm planning on having them someday, you know. This house was designed with a wife and children in mind. Didn't you realize that?" He seemed puzzled by her bewilderment.

Lindsay quickly turned away, her shoulders, sagging. "Of course, Jason. I understand. Everyone hopes to have a family someday. Somehow I had the impression that you were more of a loner than other men. You seem to appreciate quiet more, that's all. Well, as everything seems to be already set up, I must assume that congratulations are in order, or at least soon will be, right? I wish you all that you could want, Jason." She could not face him, afraid of these sudden, intense feelings of depression that had taken away the glory of the day. It was obvious to her that Marcia would soon be the wife that Jason was talking about.

"I hope your wish for me comes true, Lindsay, and that I do get everything I want. In fact, I can't think of when I wanted something so badly, so I'm going to do everything in my power to make that wish of yours come true." An enigmatic smile lit his dark countenance.

Chapter Eight

Lindsay forced a slight smile and asked Jason if she could phone her father now. He nodded and led her back to his study.

"If you'll excuse me for a few minutes, Lindsay, I'll leave you to speak to Ray. There's something I have to do outside. If you need me, call, okay?"

She nodded and his words reverberated through her now-fatigued head; *if you need me . . . if you need me . . .* But she knew now that she could never call Jason. He belonged to Marcia and they could never be more than friends. She must force herself to continue with her plan to find a life for herself. She was certain that Jason was watching over her strictly as an old friend of her father's and also because of the age-old friendship between her mother and father and Uncle Jake. Certainly he had no other reason to make certain of her comfort and safety. She was only a troubled young woman who would complicate his life with her problems.

Sighing, she picked up the phone and dialed the number of her father's private phone in his study. She assumed he would be eating lunch at his desk, as was his custom when she wasn't there to join him. She sat quietly as the connections were finally completed, and heard the receiver click.

"Hello?" Lindsay felt tears prick her eyes at the sound of her father's voice. Swallowing quickly, she moistened her lips and forced herself to speak clearly into the phone. "Hi, Dad, it's me! I figured you'd be in your study by now."

"Lindsay Sheffield, where the hell are you? Are you all right? Answer me immediately!" her father roared.

"Well, to begin with, I am perfectly fine and safe. I'm up at Uncle Jake's cabin and no one knows I'm here. I figured it was the closest thing to sanctuary that I could think of when I left. Are things pretty rough for you down there?"

He chose to ignore her question and asked rapidly, "Are you telling me that you're completely alone up there in those woods? I know that Jake is in Greece at this moment. Why, anything could happen to you!"

Lindsay interrupted his anxious question, hesitatingly. "Well, I mean, I'm not exactly alone. That is . . . Jason is here with me. He walked in and found me asleep and kind of took over. I mean—oh, it isn't coming out right at all!"

"You're damn right it isn't coming out right! Do you mean to tell me you and Jason are staying in that cabin alone together?" he demanded indignantly.

She laughed at the picture she was sure her father was envisioning. She shook her head and chuckled softly. "No, Dad, I just didn't phrase it right. Jason found me at Jake's cabin the night I arrived. I had fallen asleep and he stopped to check the cabin on his way to his house. That's where I'm phoning from now. He lives on Lake Raponda, you know that. I'm going to stay in the cabin for a while and get my thoughts straightened out. That's why I called you. I didn't want you to worry and I wanted to explain why I left in such a hurry. If you had been there, I could have told you what happened and you might have come up with a better solution than I did, but as it was, I had to come up with something fast and I couldn't endure another day in Washington after what happened."

"Well, I gathered from your note that all hell broke loose between Alec and you. He certainly got himself into a stupid mess. I never thought he could act that recklessly, especially with gambling. That boy had a fantastic future ahead of him. I certainly hope he has learned a lesson, however painful, from all this. What happened the night of the party, Lindsay? From the beginning."

As briefly and completely as she could, Lindsay told her father what had happened. She was amazed at how detached and calm her voice sounded, almost as if she were speaking about another person. Perhaps she was no longer the same person. Her feelings had changed, and *she* had somehow subtly changed. She had become stronger, more certain of herself. Her father listened patiently without interruption until she completed her story.

"Well, honey," he sighed, "I can hardly blame you for leaving. I've seen something brewing for quite a while, and I was afraid you weren't really certain of your feelings for Alec. I'm sorry this happened, but it is certainly better that all this came out before you married him. I'm only sorry you felt compelled to pay off the I.O.U.'s that Pearson gave you. You always were a soft touch when it came to the underdog. Granted, it was your money, and you may have well saved Alec from greater disgrace if word had gotten around in the political circles about his gambling, but it was a high price to pay, honey. I'm not certain I would have advised you to do it."

"It seemed the easiest way to end everything, Dad. No loose strings. I returned Alec's ring with a note. I finished it and don't want to see or hear from him again. Alec is no longer a part of my personal life and if I had to pay that money to get rid of such a painful memory, then it was well worth it."

"Well, I think you're in for a slight surprise, my dear. Alec has been hounding me to find out where you are. He says you returned his ring without an explanation. I told him quite honestly that I didn't know where you were and I did feel that, although it was none of my business, you were an unusually good judge of character. If you had decided to return his ring, then you must have had a very good reason for doing so and it was not my place to interfere. Now I have to decide what to do about the business and professional aspects of the case. Alec is a fine worker and has done well. If I fire him now, he'll be ruined and have no chance for a future here in Washington. Nor will any of my personal friends offer him employment without a recommendation from me. I hate to see the chances of a bright young man ruined by one mistake that need never happen again. I think it might be in the best interests of all concerned if I transfer him back to our home state and let him continue his work there. After a while gossip will die down and if he proves himself reliable again I'll give him another chance here. Oh, by the way, don't be surprised if you see that check you gave Pearson returned. It seems I received a few phone calls today from Pearson's editor, requesting me to drop the whole subject if I would accept the check back uncashed. Apparently they were quite put out at what Pearson tried to do to get a story on the Sheffields and were willing to forget the whole incident. I understand from Alec that he has repaid the gambling debts with the diamond ring he had given you and with the promise not to enter any private gambling games in the future." He chuckled quietly into the phone and even Lindsay couldn't help but see the humor in the situation. The very ring that he had given her with a declaration of undying love had been used so quickly to pay off his debt! She need not worry about Alec Clarke anymore. Her father would make certain he was kept quite busy back home. No doubt, he would someday marry a girl with wealthy and influential parents. But she didn't care, she considered herself lucky.

"I can't believe the newspapers came through like that, Dad! Maybe they decided Pearson went too far this time. And just perhaps he fooled with the wrong person, you old devil!"

Her father laughed. "You just may be correct, my dear! Now, how long are you going to stay up in that wilderness? I have a feeling I'm not going to have my number-one hostess on my arm for many a month! Tired of this hectic scene, aren't you, darling? This life isn't made for you, Lindsay. I don't know what one is, but lord knows, you'll never find out if you don't experiment. Live it up, darling. Do what you want to do up there. Unwind and enjoy yourself. We'll do just fine down here. Where is Jason anyway? I want to talk to him. I missed him when he stopped in a month ago."

Lindsay closed her eyes, moved by her father's understanding. She found it difficult to speak. "He's outside doing something. I really don't know what. You never told me you and Jason kept in touch after all these years!"

Casually, her father asked, "How are you two getting along, by the way?"

Lindsay twisted her lips as she tried to think of a suitable answer. "Well, he's . . . er . . . rather . . . well . . . bossy! And stubborn, and at times very arrogant." She stopped at the sound of her father's hearty roar of laughter.

"Sounds like someone I know, only she has turquoise eyes and an impish grin! You two must be a pair to watch together! Sparks and fireworks, right?"

"It isn't a laughing matter, Father, and you don't have to sound so smug! He *is* bossy and overly protective. You'd think he owned me the way he tells me what to do! I'm a grown woman and I don't need him to watch over me day and night!"

"Doesn't sound like the Jason I know. He's quiet, very much in control, and very calm. Also very good-looking, wouldn't you say, honey?"

"Don't try to deceive, Dad. He's self-centered and probably thinks he can have any woman he wants!" she answered smugly.

"And he probably has!" answered her father quietly, his laughter barely hidden.

"Well, he isn't here and this is costing him a fortune, so I'm hanging up. I don't feel like discussing Jason Mainwaring's so-called attributes any further, Dad. I'm quite certain his friendship to you is the only reason he has been kind to me so far."

111

"Oh, I'm sure," her father answered drily and chuckled again.

"Good-bye Dad. I'll call you again next week. I'm afraid if I write to you, someone will see the postmark from here and word will get to the papers that I'm up here."

"You're right, honey. You had enough exposure before this happened and now they're practically living on our doorstep trying to find out where you disappeared to!"

They spoke for a few moments longer, and Lindsay quietly hung up, smiling happily as she gazed at the phone. From the doorway she heard a soft, deep laugh. She turned sharply and frowned. Jason was standing tall and arrogant, his head thrown back in a deep laugh.

"You've been listening!" she exclaimed indignantly.

He shook his head, still smiling, and answered, "Not really. I just came in on the part about how kind I am to you. Since I now know how you really feel about me, I think I had better prove how really kind I am by feeding you. Are you ready?"

Lips held tightly together, Lindsay glared at Jason, her head held high. He was laughing at her and she could think of nothing to say in retaliation. She nodded tightly and stood up. His eyes flashed a dark light for a brief moment as he took in her proud beauty. He stood there quietly, staring at her and her heart started to pound again as she found she couldn't avoid his bold assessment of her. She could feel her senses reach out to him, and she longed to feel the slight touch of his fingertips through her hair and the touch of his hard lips on her willing ones. She parted her lips involuntarily and forced herself to say sharply, "You look like you're assessing the points of a pedigree mare!"

"I am," he answered abruptly, and walked over to take her by the elbow and direct her out of the room, a puzzled frown on her face. For a brief moment, while they had been locked in visual combat with one another, she was certain that Jason had almost been ready to swing her up into his hard arms and carry her up to his bedroom, disregarding everything. And yet, had it been her imagination? She had felt her body tingling in response to his eyes and had known at that moment that if he had come to her like some primitive Indian and carried her off, she wouldn't have resisted. When he looked at her like that, possessively and boldly, she felt only a deep heat, a passionate response, a need that she didn't understand.

She must be hungry. Her thoughts were becoming too fanciful. She refused to watch Jason as he manuevered his long body into the soft front seat of the car and expertly backed it out of the driveway. Words were not spoken until they had been on the road for about five minutes.

"How's Ray, Lindsay? Did he understand everything?" he asked matter-of-factly. Lindsay realized that Jason would never ask anything out of mere nosiness. He wanted to know because of his friendship with her father and out of concern for her own safety and well-being.

"He's fine, holding up remarkably well, considering that the press is bugging him about my disappearance. He seems to think it's a bit laughable, for some reason. He thinks the sun rises and sets in you and is glad you were here when I arrived."

"Bet that hurt to admit, didn't it?" He grinned, his eyes still on the road.

Lindsay looked out the side window and shrugged. "I'm quite sure you are perfectly aware of my father's feelings for you. It's almost as if he thinks you're his son. You must always be on your good behavior, Jason, when you see him," she added sweetly.

"Meaning that I'm always at my worst when we're together? Oh, I don't know." He pondered the point. "I can think of some very pleasant moments when we have managed to place our differences aside. Mutually pleasant, but then, you'd never agree on that either."

"All right, Jason, quit teasing me! You wouldn't bring up those . . . moments . . . if Marcia were around."

"I wouldn't bring up those 'moments' if anyone were around. It would be none of their damn business! What I choose to do is no one's business. I thought I warned you of that before, Lindsay, so stop trying to provoke me," he warned.

Lindsay decided to change the subject. She would never win a battle with Jason.

"I remember when Mother and Father and I traveled up here each fall to stay with Jake in the cabin. I remember Dad telling me the story of this road." Lindsay noted how well the car held to the curving mountain trail.

"Yes," Jason returned quietly. "New Englanders were very proud of the Molly Stark Trail and became quite upset if anyone from another state referred to it as the 'Molly Pitcher Trail.' Unknown to many was the fact that there were two Mollys—one Molly Stark and one Molly Pitcher. Each performed the same brave service to her country during the Revolutionary War."

"Yes, I remember now," Lindsay exclaimed. "When their husbands were felled by fire from the Redcoats, each picked up her fallen husband's ramrod and continued to fire the cannons. Molly Stark was wounded in the battle, but the Americans won. They named this continuous route after her, all the way through southern Vermont." Lindsay shook her head slightly. "They were certainly pioneer women in those days—always brave and willing to try the unknown. We women are too pampered these days. Maybe if we had to work side by side with our men we would forge not only a country but many a good marriage as well." She stopped talking and wondered what had made her say that.

"Wouldn't you say that in a sense you are trying the unknown, Lindsay? After all, you left the security and position you knew in Washington, left your friends, your wealth and were determined to try and start a new life. What makes you any different than those pioneer women?"

"I'm doing this for myself, Jason, not to help a husband and raise children. And besides, I don't even know how to start a fire or, for that matter, how to row a canoe. What would have happened to me if you hadn't started that fire for me the first night? Why, come to think of it, I don't even know how to split logs!" She grinned to herself.

"Well, granted, you are lacking in a few of the basics, but those can be easily remedied. I'll show you how to split wood and start a fire, although I doubt you'll feel so independent after you feel the blisters on your hands. As for canoeing, I'll take you out. Maybe we'll even do a bit of fishing since you are determined to learn the refined ways of life," he grinned as he took in her excited look.

"Would you, Jason? I mean, you're so busy and I've taken up enough of your time. But I always did want to learn how to paddle a canoe!"

"I think I can safely say that you couldn't be in more capable hands. I was practically born with a paddle in my hands—instead of the proverbial silver spoon."

"Mine was the reverse problem." Lindsay grimaced, enjoying this lighthearted bantering. "Jason, your mother must have died when I was very young because I don't remember ever seeing her."

He nodded. "Yes, she died when I was eight, Lindsay. She was the daughter of a French-Canadian man and an Indian woman. She was beautiful, as I remember, very gentle and soft-spoken. She loved this land very much and shared that love with my father. That's one of the reasons he never gave up the cabin. I was born here and grew up learning all the ways of nature. Perhaps that's why the peace and tranquility of my earlier years has affected my work so much." He grew quiet and Lindsay held her breath, hoping he would continue talking of his youth, and the young Jason she had never known.

He continued after a few moments. "A few years after my grandmother died, my French grandfather remarried and moved to France with his new French wife after their child was born. I never knew my grandfather or his second wife and child. Their grandson Etienne is my second cousin and also my best friend. He now lives in Canada and is a trapper up in Quebec's interior. I don't think anyone knows me as well as he does, except for my father.

We're very close, Etienne and I. He's very French—volatile, romantic, and yet remote."

"Etienne's planning on visiting me for some fishing and camping in the near future. I'd like you to meet him. I think the two of you would get along well. You're beautiful enough to bring out the romantic in him and yet have an air of innocence and mystery that will cause him endless misery and self-doubt! You can try out all your French cooking on him. He grows tired of my plain fare."

Lindsay laughed and he quickly took in the finely boned face before him with the laughing eyes.

They pulled into a local restaurant in Bennington and passed unnoticed into the crowded dining area. In the semi-darkness, Lindsay noted the quiet murmur of people enjoying good food and conversation. After a simple meal of steak, baked potatoes smothered with sour cream and chives, and fresh corn, they sat quietly and finished the steaming strong black coffee that had been served with homemade apple pie.

They barely spoke, enjoying the tranquility of the old restaurant, and as Lindsay sipped her second cup of coffee, Jason lit a cigarette and slowly exhaled it with obvious pleasure, a relaxed look on his face.

"Do you think this will get you by until dinner tonight?"

She glanced up at him and grinned. "I really do make a pig out of myself, don't I?"

He shook his head and smiled. "No, you are a pleasure to take out to eat. You don't pretend to be polite and pick at your food. When you're hungry, you're hungry. I was just wondering if all your appetites are as intense."

"Now Jason, you're starting again! Stop it immediately or I'll walk out of here!" She noted the black lights dancing in his eyes and swiftly kicked his shin under the table. A brief look of surprise came over his dark face as she smugly smiled at him. He inclined his head toward her, murmuring, "Another time, little one, when you aren't so well protected by all these people," and a warning smile lit his face. Standing up, he pulled her chair out for her, casually resting his hands on her shoulders, his fingers massaging her collar bone. She was certain he could feel the thread of her rapid pulse beneath her collar.

She stood up quickly and made her way out to the car, standing in the cool fall air, the sun on her face.

Jason emerged from the restaurant and opened the car door for her, settling her inside. He leaned in the window and she watched him warily. "Are you sure you don't need anything else while we're in town?" he asked.

People passed them slowly, curiously watching the young girl in the car and the dark, virile man leaning against the window. They made a fine-looking couple, looking so obviously in love that they were oblivious to the fact that they were starting to draw the attention of passersby. Lindsay looked past Jason's broad shoulders, deeply aware of his closeness, the scent of his aftershave lotion, and the opened neck of his shirt, which exposed the fine black hairs on his brown chest.

"Jason, nothing, please. Let's go. People are watching us." She squirmed uncomfortably under his bold scrutiny and he smiled and straightened, walking to the driver's side and sliding in. She sat straight, staring ahead, afraid to look at him. Damn him! He had done that deliberately. Well, she wouldn't let him know that he disturbed her so. She'd stay cool and unruffled. He hesitated another minute and finally turned the key in the ignition and the car started toward the cabin.

As they moved along, Jason was silent and Lindsay finally turned and said quietly, "Thanks for lunch, Jason. After you leave me at the cabin, will you have much to catch up on? I've taken up most of your day."

"I'll manage," he answered quietly. "You'll be all right by yourself?"

She nodded. "I have to unpack and I'm still tired. I think I'll take a nap before I do anything else."

Jason rubbed the back of his neck with firm fingers. "Sounds good to me. I still have a lot of catching up to do when I get home." At a swift glance of distress from Lindsay he smiled and shook his head, speaking quietly.

"No, little one, not because of you. I've just been putting off the more unpleasant aspects of my work. I have a lot of phone calls to make and a great many of them are to people who consider themselves quite important. I guess they are, or they couldn't afford me, anyway." He grimaced. "It'll take me days to rummage through that pile of mail and straighten things out." Lindsay watched the bronze profile with its firm jaw and black hair, that waved slightly over the collar of Jason's heavy shirt. She smiled to herself.

"You must have a secretary, Jason. Can't she handle a lot of the mail for you?" She guessed what his firm answer would be even before the words were uttered.

"No, if I'm going to know what is going on at all times, I have to keep personally in touch with all my clients. If I deal with them on a one-to-one basis, I can avoid any trouble that might crop up. Besides, as I said, they're paying me for *my* opinion, not a secretary's or a subordinate's," he answered firmly.

"In other words, you want to stay in complete control at all times, despite the paperwork!"

Jason turned swiftly and caught the impish grin that was quickly fading from Lindsay's animated face. She looked like a cat that had caught a canary and released it unharmed. She was laughing at him and he knew it. He looked into her laughing eyes, his dark face stoic and unreadable. She sobered and wondered if she had gone too far. She remembered with a burning in the pit of her stomach the last time she had tested how far she could push Jason Mainwaring. Her full lips trembled as she watched his eyes move down to her curving mouth, aware that he had stopped the car. Nervously, Lindsay moistened her lips and forced herself to look out the side window. Her heart was pounding, and the air in the enclosed car was becoming increasingly harder to breathe. Just when she felt she could no longer stay in the confined space with Jason's warmth so near to her, she realized that they were parked in front of the cabin. With a quick intake of breath, she glanced sharply at Jason.

His mouth was twisted slightly in a teasing smile and his dark eyes were now dancing. Black lights flashed from them as he whispered huskily, "Your naiveté is astounding, Lindsay. Remember I'm not the innocent in this car. You are and I've warned you before about that tongue of yours getting you into trouble. Now, was there something else you wanted to say? I'll be more than happy to sit here and carry on a discussion with you. I'm very comfortable."

As if to prove that point, he reached into his breast pocket and took out a cigarette, lighting it with casual ease, a half-smile on his face. Lindsay tightened her lips in anger, knowing that once again Jason had had the last word. How dare he laugh at her?

She quickly stepped from the car and before slamming the door, leaned down and said through taut lips, her cheeks stained with color, "You are the supreme egotist, Jason Mainwaring. You may think you're the answer to every woman's dreams, but you're certainly not the answer to this one's!" Stiffly, she threw her long hair over her shoulder and turned and walked up the steps with pride. As she inserted the key into the lock, she heard Jason drive slowly away, not waiting to make certain that she got in the house safely. She frowned, aware of a sense of vague disappointment. She had been afraid that he would follow her into the cabin after her last remark, and now that he hadn't, and had so casually driven away, Lindsay felt no relief, only a sense of uneasiness and disquiet. She brushed a slim hand through her dark hair and lifted her chin into the air. The hell with Jason. She had come here to be on her own and that was just what she was going to do!

She walked into the bedroom and heatedly kicked off her shoes. As she lay down on the bed, she remembered another bedroom, more spacious and more beautifully appointed, and pounded a fist into the pillow. Damn him! Must she think of him constantly? He either irritated her or bemused her. She could never be oblivious to the feelings that were aroused deep within her whenever she was around Jason. He was the kind of person a woman either loved or hated and she refused to allow herself to even think of him as anything other than Jake's son and a friend of her father. She had her own life to straighten out.

She had left one man and was not about to become involved with another, especially one like Jason. He had some irresistible force that aroused an answering emotion in her. Sometimes, like now, that emotion was one of anger and frustration, but it was the other emotion that frightened her. The feeling of complete surrender and unfulfillment that he awakened in her with the slightest touch, and at times with a certain somnolent look. He was the only man who had ever made her aware of the fact that she was a woman, and she resented his dominance over her emotions. Jason was right. She was an innocent in the ways of love. Only the love that he was speaking of was timeless, a primitive and turbulent surge of unrelenting passion between male and female, something as basic and old as time itself. She wasn't prepared to cope with it.

Refusing to think further on the traitorous subject, Lindsay got out of bed, unable to sleep, and walked into the spare bedroom. Picking up her sketches, she carried them into the living room and methodically studied each one. Pleased, she decided to start on colored chalk sketches tomorrow.

Lindsay turned the page of her pad and casually started to doodle lines on the blank page as she thought of the amount of work she would have to put in this week in order to catch the vivid colors of the changing country before frost hit the area in a few weeks. A slight smile formed on her lips as she continued drawing careless lines, some bold, some slightly shaded in, not concentrating on what her charcoal pencil was producing on the paper.

Her thoughts were filled with the work to be done and the enjoyment and peace that it gave her. She could almost picture the finished oils of the waterfall, as it tumbled down to a creek surrounded by bursts of vibrant fall colors. Placing the pencil aside, she casually glanced down at the now-filled page. She swallowed and stared in amazement at the pad. Without thinking she had drawn a bold likeness of Jason Mainwaring. His pride and arrogance were easily seen in the few brief bold lines that her pencil had made. And his face, dark and dangerous, seemed to laugh up at her.

Chapter Nine

The following week passed quietly for Lindsay. She tried to concentrate on her work, spending the warm fall days in the woods, drawing and sketching in colored chalks the wonders that constantly challenged her ability as an artist. She now had no doubt as to what she wanted to do with her life.

She could definitely see the rapid improvement that she was making in her work as she spent longer and later hours, rarely stopping for food or thought. She had forced all thoughts of Jason out of her mind, thowing herself into her work, forcing herself to concentrate on the sketched canvases before her. She worked feverishly, learning by instinct as the days quickly passed. Lindsay was now certain that she had a natural talent and love for painting. The natural talents of a true and gifted artist, which had been hidden deep within her, were now released. She was pleased with herself, and certain that she could develop a career in art if she studied and worked long and hard enough. Uncle Jake had been right all those years. He had seen in her what had been hidden from others—not her external beauty, but the deeply private and sensitive person that Lindsay really was.

Toward the end of the week, as she was waking up one morning, she heard the sound of tires in the driveway. Her heart stopped as she found herself hoping it might be Jason. She rapidly brushed her hair and threw on a heavy sweater and some old jeans. Quickly pulling on a pair of wool socks and sneakers, she ran to answer the heavy pounding on the door. She threw open the door and the smile that had formed on her full lips froze.

Lindsay stared at the older man standing there before her. He was wearing workman's clothes, and in his hand he held some papers.

She felt her throat close in momentary fear that he recognized her as he stood there staring at her, a frown on his face. Lindsay forced her voice to sound nonchalant and gazed at the man coolly. "May I help you?" She forced her eyes to meet his pale blue ones with confidence.

A work-worn hand held out the papers. His face was creased with a puzzled frown as he asked in a nasal voice with a strong New England accent, "Pardon, miss. Is this here Jason Mainwaring's cabin?"

Lindsay nodded silently, her lips held tightly together.

"Well, that's good. Sure would've hated to make this trip fur nothin', ya know. Time's important! I got orders here to install the telephone and I'm ready if I could get to work, ma'am?"

"The telephone?" Lindsay questioned. The older man screwed up his eyes and shook his head, as if her question was typical of the simple kind that women always asked when a man had work to do.

"Yes, miss. The telephone that Mr. Mainwaring ordered last week." He glanced quickly at the papers in his gnarled hand. "Everything here looks okay. Unlisted phone for this cabin. Party's name, Jason Mainwaring. Look, miss, I ain't got time to stand around. There's other places I got to go to today and this'll only take a short time. Sorry if I interrupted your day, but I'll work as fast as I can."

Lindsay smiled briefly and opened the door to admit the man. A telephone! How dare Jason! He knew she wanted privacy. Now there would be a direct connection between his house and the cabin. Furious, she drummed her fingertips on the table as she bit her lips in anger. He knew she

123

could never refuse the phone. It would only cause the telephone repairman to become suspicious and he might start asking her questions. Her thoughts were interrupted as she heard the man talking to her.

"Where do you want the phone installed, ma'am? Instructions don't state where the location is to be, only that it's to be a desk phone." He looked around the cabin, perplexed.

"Over there, please." Lindsay pointed toward the table against the wall in the living room. The man nodded his gray head and moved the old table away from the wall. Placing his toolbox by his side, he proceeded to work quietly and efficiently.

Lindsay watched the man working and after a short while offered him some coffee. When he agreed, she ran to the kitchen and soon returned with a coffee tray. She quietly handed him a mug, steaming hot and strong, and sat in the chair to continue to watch him work.

"You sure do make a good cup of coffee, miss. Hits the spot now that fall's here, ya know?" He concentrated on attaching some wires into the wall plate and Lindsay smiled, silently berating herself for what she now considered a foolish fear that this local man would recognize her. She had just now realized that she was becoming less and less afraid that someone might recognize her. It was almost as if it didn't matter as much anymore. She was slowly finding herself, and was unafraid of what other people might expect of her. She was finding her own strength and in that her own feelings of security in being herself.

As the man tidied up the area and replaced the table against the wall, he straightened and picked up his toolbox. "You are one of the prettiest young gals I've seen in a long time in these parts, young 'un. Hope you ain't just plannin' on passin' through after the leaves fall. Our winters can be mighty cold up this ways, but a fine-lookin' gal like you must have a boy that can keep you warm. You have the look of an outsider, but I think there's more steel in you than that bony outside shows.

"Well, that's all I got to say. Got to be on with my work. Thanks again for that coffee. Make someone a mighty good wife, mighty good."

Lindsay grinned as she followed the older man to the door and saw him into his truck. She waved as he turned and gave her a wink and grin. She shook her head in laughter and disbelief. What a way to start the morning. What was it that she had always heard? New Englanders never said anything unless it was important enough to say, and now this old sage had her married off! She laughed again, and then frowned slightly. Getting married was the last thing she wanted, if the old man only knew! She was free and independent now and no man was going to tie her down to wait on him, to carry out his slightest whim. She had narrowly escaped that with Alec and she wasn't about to let it happen again!

For some reason her traitorous thoughts formed the figure of a tall, lean man, vital and healthy, arrogant and full of pride. Again she saw a bronzed face, diamond-bright eyes amused and questioning, as if they saw something in her that she herself refused to admit. Damn Jason. The attraction that Jason held was purely a sexual one, a naturally physical attraction that was common between a good-looking man and a vulnerable girl like herself. She must recognize it as only that and try to deal with it in a logical and realistic way.

There was Marcia to consider. She obviously thought she was going to marry Jason. She had made that clear enough in her demonstration of her possession of him that day when she had met Lindsay. They'll make a beautiful pair, Lindsay thought sarcastically.

Determined to think no more of Jason, she tried to ignore the tiny question that kept repeating itself in the deeper recesses of her mind. Why hadn't Jason come over all this week? Why hadn't he even tried to make certain that everything was all right here?

She did battle with her thoughts. What did she care anyway? She got what she wanted when she had last seen him; he had stopped bothering her with his "big brother concern." And yet, she missed him, missed the way he made her laugh. Her feelings were paradoxical, ambivalent, and she was confused because one moment she found herself hating Jason for his lordly strength and overbearing ways, but at the same time, she found it difficult to assimilate the deeper, instinctive emotions that he had awakened in her.

Frowning, Lindsay tossed her long hair over her shoulder and swallowed the last of her coffee. She noticed the fireplace and glanced at the log tray. There was almost no wood left. She had been so happy each night, carefully making a fire with twigs and newspapers that she had found in a back shed that she had failed to realize that she was quickly consuming the wood that had already been split.

She straightened her shoulders with determination. Well, if she could make a fire on her own, she could cut more wood for any future fires she needed. She didn't need Jason to oversee that!

Putting on her wool jacket and gloves, Lindsay walked to the back of the cabin and stomped over the brush to the shed. Inside she found a heavy iron wedge and a sledgehammer. She lifted them with difficulty, carried them outside, and dropped them near a square cemented area.

From the oversized woodpile, she hauled out the smallest log she could find, amazed at its weight and diameter. She had always envisioned the splitting of logs to be a fairly easy job, at least, when she had seen it done as a child, Jake had always made it look easy.

Huffing with exertion, she carried the heavy log over to the cement and stood it upright. Determined to succeed, she lifted up the heavy sledgehammer in one hand and held the iron wedge against the middle of the log.

She remembered that she had to tap the wedge into the center of the log before she could split the entire piece with one whack of the sledgehammer. With great difficulty she managed to hold the heavy weight of the hammer in one hand and the wedge steady with the other. She rationalized that perhaps she was having so much trouble because her hands didn't have the strength that was needed. Or perhaps, she thought wryly, she actually needed four hands.

Finally the wedge was set and Lindsay lifted the huge, long hammer, ready to strike the blow that would split the log in one fell swoop.

Her blow missed, hitting the log and causing it to tumble over. In frustration, she righted the log and once again swung the heavy hammer, this time with success. The blow hit the iron wedge and forced it into the log one more inch.

Lindsay stared in disgust at the small amount of success she had to show for such a great effort, and in anger once again swung the hammer, this time forcing the wedge halfway into the hard log. In disbelief, she stood there, sweating and trying to catch her breath. With one more try, she swung the hammer as hard as she could, a determined grimace on her face. As she hit the wedge she closed her eyes and said a quick prayer. She opened her eyes, prepared to see a log split in two and ready for her fireplace, but what she saw caused her to let out a yell of rage and kick the still standing log. The wedge was deeply imbedded in the center of the log, and she knew there was no way on earth she could remove it. The sun poured down on her body and she tore off her jacket in deep frustration and rage at her weakness. Her breasts strained against the sweater as she tried to catch her breath. Slumping down beside the log, she stared at it in bewilderment, her arms thrown over her bent legs, and shook her head. It had always seemed so easy when her father or Jake had done it. Surely she must have done something wrong. Now what would she do? She had been so certain she could manage, and here she was, feeling sorry for herself because she couldn't even split a stupid log!

Suddenly she became aware of a long, dark shadow on the ground before her, and she knew instinctively from the softness of the tread that it was Jason. Lindsay glanced up over her shoulder, resentment seething in her that he should find her like this. The darkening blaze from her now stormy blue-green eyes dared him to say something derogatory.

He stood there, still and dark, his bronze face bland, taking in her still-heaving breasts and angry eyes. Her quivering lips seemed close to tears as she tightened them.

Without saying a word, Jason walked over to the woodshed. Lindsay just sat on the ground, refusing to give him the satisfaction of asking for help, and watched him as he walked over and handed her a slim, round length of wood. She reached up for it, a question in her eyes.

"Here, hold that steady directly over the iron wedge with both hands and don't move. Close your eyes, Lindsay."

She opened her mouth to object and quickly bit her lips, realizing that there was hardly anything she could say under the circumstances. She knelt down and did as Jason instructed. Her eyes widened in momentary fear as she saw him lift the sledgehammer effortlessly over his broad shoulder and bring it down. She squeezed her eyes shut and heard a crash. Quickly, she glanced down to see the split log. The stick of wood had forced the wedge on through the log and had freed it.

She took in a deep breath and forced herself to say, "I suppose now you'll tell me I was foolish to try and do this and that a woman's place is in the kitchen." She refused to look up at him and struggled to stand, feeling disgruntled and messy.

"I might," he drawled softly, "but I think it's commendable that you're determined to be independent. But there comes a fine line, honey, between wanting to be independent and being downright stubborn." He noted the mutinous expression on her face. Her eyes watched him warily as she once again saw those black lights start to dance in his eyes. She felt grimy and disheveled suddenly, and was very much aware of Jason's clean male scent as he stood near to her, dressed in tight jeans and a pullover sweater. He looked clean, vital and right where he belonged, standing firmly on this New England soil. Unconsciously, Lindsay drew a slim hand through her hair and pulled it away from her face. For some reason she could not force her eyes away from his. They seemed to hold her, to force her to listen to his words.

"I'm the first one to admit that you are not the type who loves little garden luncheons, or society teas, Lindsay, and I'm all for you doing what you want. But you've got to take it slowly. You're pushing yourself to the extreme, trying to prove to yourself that you can do everything on your own. No one can do that. Everyone needs someone else, and that is something you're going to have to learn no matter how long it takes."

She interrupted him. "And you, Jason, are you telling me that you, of all people, need someone, even for part of the time?" She could have bitten her tongue when she said it, but the thought of Marcia had come between them and she had to know.

He looked down at her from his great height and took in her small frame, hands thrust in her jeans' pockets, head thrown back proudly. Once again that bland expression closed his face to her as he answered her with a slight half-smile.

"Perhaps I might surprise you, Lindsay, but I might even need *someone* all of the time," he said. His head tilted to one side as he observed her sudden look of discomfiture.

"Now, I have a surprise for you. Why don't you go in and take a shower and change your clothes and I'll finish up the job you started. That was one of the reasons I came over today. I thought I'd give you the week to get settled in and figured you would be ready for a break about now." He picked up the sledgehammer with little effort and proceeded to split the rest of the wood with an ease that Lindsay mistakenly had thought she could duplicate. He ignored her presence and she finally spoke, excitement in her voice.

"What kind of clothes should I change into and just

where you are taking me now, Jason? I'm not going anywhere until you tell me. And another thing. What's the big idea of putting a phone in the cabin? I admit that maybe taking on the woodpile was a little bit out of my line, and required more strength than I have, but you could have asked me if I wanted a phone. Now I suppose you'll be calling me every night to tuck me into bed by phone!"

Jason stopped his work and carefully placed the sledgehammer on the ground, holding the handle next to his lean hip as he said softly, "Believe me, Lindsay, if I was going to tuck you into bed each night, *I* wouldn't do it over the phone. The reason I had the phone installed was to allow you to phone your father whenever you chose. I think he'd like to hear how you're doing, don't you? And besides, I don't like the idea of you being here alone in case of an emergency. The phone stays. Now go get into a clean pair of jeans and another sweater. You won't need anything else. I'm taking you for a ride in my canoe."

Lindsay's crestfallen face suddenly lit up and she gazed up at Jason with joy radiating from her face. She impulsively threw her arms around his neck and squeezed him tightly. It wasn't until she felt the sudden heat radiating between them that she tensed, aware that her sudden impulsiveness had unearthed hidden emotions between them. She froze, unable to pull herself away from him, starting to tremble, afraid of what might happen next as she heard the sledgehammer slip to the hard ground with a thud. She felt Jason tighten his hands around her waist and hold them there for a brief moment. She was certain that he could feel the quickness of her heartbeat through her thin sweater. He seemed to withdraw into himself, and she felt his chest rise as he inhaled deeply. With a firm but deliberate move he pushed her away from him slowly, his face dark and unreadable.

She had wanted him to kiss her, and she knew that for one moment he had almost given way to his instinct, but something had stopped him. Her cheeks flamed brightly as she realized that he was probably thinking of Marcia. She bit her lip and nodded, eyes downcast.

"Thank you, Jason. It was kind of you to think that I might want to go canoeing. I appreciate your thoughtfulness. I'll go and change." She turned and ran into the cabin, feeling like a stupid schoolgirl.

As she washed her hair and quickly dried it, pulling it back into a braid, she began to feel less foolish and more excited about the outing. Perhaps Jason might even let her paddle the canoe.

When she was ready, she walked out into the living room to see Jason straightening up from the fireplace. A pile of split logs lay to the side, enough to last for a good week, and she was sure there was an equal amount out in the shed. He smiled and nodded in approval of her outfit.

"I get the distinct impression, young lady, that you're more than excited about this surprise. How long have you actually wanted to do this?"

She laughed and said, "Ever since I was a kid. There's not much call for canoe rides in Washington!"

Jason's teeth showed white as he threw back his dark head in laughter. "Come on, let's get on with it, novice. You got a lot to learn!"

Lindsay glanced at him from beneath veiled lashes. No, he wasn't insinuating anything about her inexperience this time. In fact, he seemed to enjoy having the chance to teach her.

"Are you sure I don't need a jacket or something?"

"No, the sun is warm today, and you'll get quite hot out here on the water. Take your sunglasses if you want, although you might lose them if the canoe tips."

Lindsay shook her head. "I'll take the view in its natural coloring, thank you. I'm not going to spoil the scenery with shades!"

Jason reached out to grasp Lindsay's wrist as she went by him. He glanced down at his watch and asked, "I don't know how long we'll be gone. Did you eat breakfast?"

She shrugged and answered, "I'm fine, Jason, really. Us lumberjacks always eat a hearty breakfast before we go to work! Come on, I don't want to miss one moment of this glorious weather!" She grinned and reached out for his hand, suddenly hesitant that he might cancel their outing if she mentioned that she had wakened that morning with a sore throat and slight aching in her chest. She felt that a cold was coming on and was ruefully aware that the morning's tryout with the sledgehammer hadn't eased her aching muscles any. She hadn't had a chance to eat that morning, but she really didn't feel hungry. Quickly, she dismissed all thoughts that might dampen her adventure with Jason. She had waited so long for this and it suddenly seemed most important to her that Jason had taken the time to think of her to take her out and do something that he thought she might enjoy.

As she settled in the comfortable front seat of Jason's car, she listened as Jason explained where they would be canoeing. Before long, they pulled into the driveway of his house. She turned and gave him a questioning glance.

"Well, it's time to get out and exercise those city-bred legs of yours, Lindsay. I've no doubt that they've always looked spectacular in sheer silk stockings and thin sandals, but this is the country now and you're going to have to build up muscles that you never thought you had, let alone use! We have a short walk to the lake where I keep the canoe."

Lindsay tilted her head sideways and asked warily, "Just how long will this walk take, Jason? Are you deliberately putting something over on me? Like, for instance, teaching the determined city gal a lesson she won't forget?" She got out of the car and planted her feet stubbornly in the gravel driveway. She didn't trust him. He looked like he was having too good a time, and possibly at her expense! Her tiny chin jutted out mutinously as she waited for his answer.

"Now, would I do something like that to you, a sophisticated and beautiful woman of the world?" Jason climbed out of the car and walked toward her. "You wanted to try new things, and believe me, this is an experience you won't forget. You were just dying to jump into that canoe and start paddling, weren't you?"

At her brief nod, she saw his lips quirk slightly in a hidden smile as he continued. "Well, first of all, there are a few rules. I promised you a ride in my canoe—a ride, Lindsay. That does not mean you're going to step in, sit down, and start learning how to paddle. It's a tricky business, believe me. You'll have to do exactly as I say, when I say it. I know that goes against your grain because I can see the sparks in your eyes already, but that's the way it is. Let's just say you're inexperienced and it's my ballgame and my ball. If you don't want to play it my way, I'll just take my ball and go home." He chuckled as he saw her bite down on her bottom lip to stifle a swift retort.

Damn him, Lindsay thought. He knows how much I'm looking forward to this! Why does he have to treat me like a child and give me this boy scout lesson? He's deliberately teasing me and I won't give him the satisfaction by blowing up again.

She gave Jason a sweet smile and said sarcastically, "Really, Jason, you'd think we were back in the 1800s and you were an Indian and I was nothing but your squaw that you give orders to. Well, I'm not your squaw and I'm more than willing to concede that you know more about canoeing than I do. But that doesn't mean that I'm incapable of learning, you know!" She felt very satisfied that she had not given in to his teasing.

Jason watched her from his great height, arms folded, and softly answered, "May I make one minor point, honey? In the 1800s an Indian and his squaw were equal partners, regardless of what your movies and television may have taught you. A canoe was essential for survival in those days, for hunting and fishing, and no Indian ever took as his squaw a woman who wasn't willing or one who couldn't pull her own weight. They were a team; they depended on each other and I feel the same way. No one has ever paddled that canoe except Etienne, and I don't feel inclined to relinquish my last great freedom in this so-called civilized world by allowing a woman to go paddling *my* canoe, that *I* built, all over *my* lake, whenever the Susan B. Anthony mood hits her! It's *my* last private sanctuary, the place where I can be alone with my thoughts. It's my world, Lindsay. Do you understand now? Today I extended an invitation to you, not an offer to teach you the skills of canoeing."

Lindsay's eyes darkened into a midnight blue as she whispered with incredulity, "Why, Jason Mainwaring, you're nothing but a twentieth-century throwback! You belong two hundred years ago! All this stuff you've been handing me about finding myself and doing what I really wanted to is a bunch of hogwash! If you honestly felt that way, you'd never say the things you just did!"

"Lindsay, you're not listening. As usual, you hear just what you want to. I meant every word I said to you. I want you to be happy and one has nothing to do with the other. I'm just pointing out that as much as you love your privacy and feel out of place in the world you left in Washington, there are times that I feel the same, perhaps even more strongly." He squinted his dark eyes and took in her stormy look and stance. Suddenly he chuckled deeply, a husky sound that caused her heart to beat more quickly and a slight stirring in the pit of her stomach. She realized that Jason was still as attractive to her as always, no matter how angry or frustrated with him she became.

"Perhaps you're right, little one. Maybe I should have been born a few hundred years ago. Who knows. I might have even dragged you off with me to share the wild, untamed wilderness. Yes," he mused, "I might even have offered you my paddle." He straightened and smiled benignly. "But of course, the time is now, and I am much older than you and much too decadent. I've lived longer and experienced more than you, and you're still my little cousin and I'm here to watch over you, aren't I? So let's go." He drew off a light jacket and threw it over his shoulder and took her by the elbow, as they walked toward the lake.

Lindsay concentrated on the ground beneath her feet

but her mind was wandering wildly. Her breath had stopped in her throat when Jason had made that remark about dragging her off with him. She had forced her eyes away from his gaze, unwilling to let him see the light that had suddenly appeared in them at his statement. A light of hope? Oh lord, that's all she needed now, to start thinking that Jason might look upon her as someone other than a girl that needed his protection. Her mind wandered and she saw herself, following Jason through the woods, dressed as a squaw in leather. The vision brought a smile to her lips. Her mind abruptly returned to the present as she bumped into Jason's hard frame. She looked up in surprise as she realized they had come to the edge of the lake. Jason was pointing to a long shed, the wood a colorless gray, made dull by the elements.

Jason walked proudly over to the open end of the shed and walked inside. Lindsay decided to stay where she was after the lecture she had just received. If he needed help, he could ask for it, she thought. She watched as Jason slowly walked out of the shed, an apparently very light birch canoe held over his head. She observed the smile of satisfaction on his bronze face and couldn't help appreciating his apparent pleasure.

He turned the canoe over and she walked over to it, staring at the fine craftsmanship. Jason had said he had made the canoe himself, and she could see where he had fitted each finely hewn split of birch, slotting them together. She had remembered from a documentary that she had once seen on canoe-making that after the easily bendable birch was shaped and tarred and tied, it was set in water to swell the wood, thus closing any gaps in the wood seams and making the canoe watertight. She shook her head in admiration, a small smile playing around her lips.

"You seem to like what you see, Lindsay. What are you thinking?" She told him what she had seen on television and he nodded, running his dark hand through his straight hair.

"Jason, where are the boards for the seats?"

"Most true birch Indian canoes don't have them.

They're quite rounded, as you can see, and you either kneel or sit in them cross-legged. That way they don't tip over. That was why I mentioned that you would have to do exactly as I told you. I didn't think that your idea of a real canoe coincided with mine. Whether you kneel or sit in the front, Lindsay, remember this. Whatever happens, I don't want you to move your body. Any change of position could tip us right over. Perhaps you'd feel more comfortable just sitting cross-legged?"

She nodded, and asked, "But which is the front?"

Jason laughed. "There is no front or back. They're both the same. I'll sit in the back and do the paddling. You just enjoy the view up front, okay? Come on, ready to give it a try?"

She nodded, excited, and cautiously held onto the sides of the canoe as Jason steadied it in the water. Placing one foot at a time into the rounded bottom of the canoe, she eventually wriggled her slim frame into a seated position, still holding onto the sides. It rocked and rolled slightly from side to side as Jason stepped in, and Lindsay slowly turned her head, just enough to see Jason place himself into a kneeling position, paddle in hand.

She could see now why Jason had been so vehement about her not moving while they were in the water. She was gripping the sides so tightly that her knuckles grew taut and white. Her stomach churned and she bit her lip, wondering if this had been such a great idea. Well, she thought wryly, I'm in it now and I'll be darned if I'm going to shout chicken to Jason!

"You all right, Lindsay?" Forcing herself to stare straight ahead and not move her body, she nodded carefully, removing her hands and grasping her crossed legs with them. She could almost feel Jason's all-knowing smile beaming down at her from the back of the canoe. He knew damn well how she felt!

As he pushed off from the edge of the lake and maneuvered the canoe out into the deeper waters, Lindsay grasped the sides once again. No matter what happened while they were out in the lake, she vowed she would not give Jason the satisfaction of saying "I told you so." She would sit in this position all day if it killed her. Already, because of the aching in her shoulders and back, a reminder of her firewood fiasco, she was beginning to regret her determination to show Jason that she could take anything he could dish out.

Chapter Ten

━━━

Lindsay drew the back of her hand across her forehead and squinted up into the hot October sun that was beating down on her exposed head. She had no idea how long she had been seated in the front of the canoe but she was becoming increasingly aware of the heat of the day, particularly since Jason had insisted that she wear the lightweight canvas life jacket that was slipped through her arms and hung over her back.

She had insisted that she could swim like a fish but in his typical stoical manner he had coolly resisted her attempts to change his mind and had practically placed the slight jacket over her back himself. She had begrudgingly given in because she wanted the canoe trip and knew that he would have refused to take her if she didn't comply with his instructions.

The life jacket now lay heavy on her back, warmed by the sun, and she could feel the perspiration trickling down her back. The reflection from the hot sun off the cold and clear waters increased the sensations of heat encasing her body.

They had circled a portion of the lake and she guessed that they had been sliding through the crystal waters about two hours. Jason had hardly said anything to her during the entire time. She could well see why he felt so quiet during the ride. She herself had experienced the calming effect of the lake, with the only sound the lapping of Jason's paddle as he skillfully propelled the canoe through the peaceful mountain waters. Occasionally the hawking or trill of some hidden bird could be heard overhead, but for the most part there was only silence.

The autumn colors and the cloudless blue sky made an unforgettable picture, and she wished she could sketch the scene. Lindsay had long since forgotten her fear of tipping over, and had grown accustomed to the slight sideward roll of the canoe.

By now her legs and back were becoming increasingly cramped and she was becoming restless to change her position. She had insidiously tried to slide her long legs from their lotus position and kneel like Jason was doing, but her squirming had brought an abrupt reprimand from her dark companion.

She had immediately grimaced and stifled the sharp words that were so quick to come to her lips whenever Jason ordered her around. Instead, she drew a deep breath and resolved once again not to let Jason Mainwaring know how uncomfortable she had become. Her head jerked up as she heard his quiet words.

"We're almost back at the landing, Lindsay. You'll be able to stretch as soon as I pull up to the edge of the lake. Just stay with me a little longer. You've done just fine."

She refused to allow herself to smile at his unexpected praise. She relaxed a little, calm in the knowledge that she would soon be on dry land and could move around. She turned her head slowly and recognized certain parts of the lake edge that she knew belonged to Jason. All she wanted right now was a long, hot bath to ease her aching muscles and something icy cold to drink to relieve the soreness and dryness of her parched throat. Strangely enough, she didn't feel hungry, despite her usually hearty appetite. She attributed that to the slight nausea she felt from the rolling of the canoe.

Suddenly, from overhead, Lindsay heard a loud, piercing noise, the honking of a large grouping of Canadian

geese flying south. Enthralled at the beauty of their forma-
tion and colors, she followed their quick flight overhead
through the blue sky and with a delighted laugh, threw her
arm up and turned her body quickly to watch their departure.

"Look, Jason! Aren't they beautiful?" Her words were
hardly out of her mouth when she heard a sharp command from Jason to sit still. But it was too late. She could
already feel the heavy roll of the canoe, thrown to one
side by her quick movement, and with a gasp, she grabbed
hold of the sides to gain her balance. She heard Jason
cursing quietly to himself and had no doubts that she was
the cause of his sudden verbal assault. He was working the
paddle furiously, but Lindsay felt a sudden sense of fore-
boding as she realized the canoe was keeling over. She and
Jason were dumped unceremoniously into the icy waters
of the lake.

Sputtering, she quickly came to the surface, and looked
around for Jason, trying to call his name. He was busy
forcing the lightweight canoe upright. As Lindsay saw the
paddle float toward her, she grabbed it, treading water.
Jason's eyes, now black with a strange, flashing light of
deep rage, lighted on her and he motioned for her to swim
to the shore. Suddenly afraid of the look on his face, one
that she had never seen before, Lindsay swam like the
devil was trailing her. Jason was swiftly maneuvering the
canoe from behind and kicking his long legs through the
cold water. Lindsay's heart thumped with fear of what
Jason would say or do. She drew herself up to the shore,
dragged her sodden legs through the last few feet of water,
and continued to walk a few more feet over the stone surface of the shoreline.

Shrugging off the life jacket, she turned and watched
Jason pull the canoe up over the stones onto dry land. She
stood there, unable to move, holding her breath as she
watched him. He looked like some pagan water god,
emerging dark and relentless from the water. He ripped
off the soaking sweater and threw it to the ground in disgust. Lindsay grimaced and then caught her breath, find-

ing herself unable to breathe as he turned toward her, his bronze chest wet, covered with thick black hairs, and rapidly drying in the heat of the sun. She couldn't take her eyes from his.

They held her pinned to the spot where she stood, her hand still holding the paddle and her long hair gleaming as black as his and dripping in her face. She unconsciously reached up and pushed the wet hair from her face. She was totally unaware of her own wet clothes, nor was she aware of being cold. The sun was hot, but not as hot as the blazing anger that was directed at her from Jason.

His fiery gaze glanced down at the thin, wet sweater clinging to her now heaving breasts as she stood rooted to the spot like a frightened doe that knows it's being hunted by a predator. Lindsay was aware of the ineffectuality of her thin silk and lace bra. She knew she looked naked and it only made her more breathless as she saw a certain determination cross Jason's face and watched as his black eyes suddenly became veiled behind long, dark lashes.

This was a Jason she had never met, a true primitive standing there in the sun, bronze chest heaving as he tried to catch his breath after his efforts with the canoe. But there was something else different about him. It was as if they had been thrown back into time, into another place. He looked every bit like one of his Indian ancestors, dangerous, ruthless, and totally unpredictable.

Lindsay felt her legs move instinctively, working themselves backward and up over the stony edge toward the pine trees that framed the lake. Her mouth moved wordlessly, her eyes stormy blue and pleading to this stranger who was now softly and slowly stalking her with purposeful, long strides. She tried to think of something to say, anything to bring back the Jason that she had known, but her mind wouldn't work. Nothing would stop this man. His anger was directing him, his anger and something more primeval, a basic instinct that was driving him toward her, his eyes flicking over her trembling body. She was trembling in fear, and because of something else deep within her that she did not care to define. Something was happening to them both and Lindsay recognized that she had never felt like this before. She was still afraid of Jason, of *this* Jason, yet she felt an unexplainable thrill. She placed her hands, still shaking, in front of her and pleaded with him.

"Jason, please stop. I'm sorry. I didn't think when I saw the geese flying overhead. I only wanted to share them with you!" She faltered. He wasn't listening to her, just moving forward, intent on his destination. She turned suddenly, the fear overtaking her, and started to run, her legs feeling like jelly. She went about two feet when a hard grip around her ankle flipped her to the ground, soft and covered with pine needles from a giant, dark pine overhead.

She turned over and gazed up at him, standing over her, tall and forbidding, his feet firmly planted on the ground. Her lips trembled as she gazed up at Jason, her eyes afraid, excited, her emotions playing havoc with her. Jason stood there, hands on his hips, staring intently down at her as she tried to speak again, explain—anything! Her gaze swung to the fine dark hairs on the large expanse of his chest, and she swallowed and ran the tip of her tongue over her lips to moisten them. Her breath felt constricted and she couldn't move, held prisoner by the intensity of his dark eyes. He spoke, his voice coming with a deep, soft huskiness that she had never heard before.

"I warned you more than once, Lindsay, to never provoke me or you would pay the consequences. This time you've gone too far, and I'm not in a very forgiving mood. This time you're going to pay, honey. You might even enjoy it, even if you do think I'm a chauvinistic throwback. I'm slow to burn, Lindsay, but when I finally do blow up, the fire burns and consumes very quickly!"

With an angry shriek, Lindsay tried to scramble away, but Jason was too quick for her. He grabbed her by the shoulders and pinned her to the soft warm ground as they struggled together. Try as she could, Lindsay couldn't squirm from under the weight of his long body, and eventually he had her pinned beneath him. He held her arms above her head as his chest pressed her into the sweet, pine-smelling ground below.

Her legs twisted ineffectually from side to side but his lean, hard hips held her own hips firmly. Fury came trembling through her voice as she realized the advantage his huge frame held over her own slim one.

"Jason, you wouldn't dare . . ." Her words were immediately stopped as his firm lips descended to hers. Just before they touched hers, she heard him whisper, "I do dare . . ."

His mouth felt like a fiery brand—hard, unrelenting, demanding and possessive. She struggled against his ruthless onslaught, outraged by the force and brutality of his kiss. The hard mouth lifted slightly and dark eyes stared directly into her own, a different light in them now. Then his firm mouth took her lips again, only this time in a vastly different manner. They teased softly, moving back and forth over her own, forcing her mouth to relax. It was a soft, sensual kiss that seduced her with its indolence. Devastating and potent, and totally irresistible, it caused her to respond, slowly at first, her lips parting of their own volition, allowing Jason to release her arms so that she could place them around his strong neck.

Lindsay felt inertia coming over her. A warmth was spreading through her body, and she stopped struggling. She was intensely aware of Jason's hard length as he fitted himself tightly over her. She reveled in the excitement she felt surge through her as his lips parted her own with more strength and his tongue investigated the sweetness of her mouth more thoroughly. Her fingers worked their way through his hair and down to his throat. She could feel the wild beating of his heart at her fingertips and was certain that its rapid beat matched her own.

Her body felt on fire and as her fingers reached the fine, furry expanse of his chest and instinctively caressed him, she heard him moan deeply in his throat. He pulled her closer to him, wrapping his strong arms around her. She could feel his hard legs press against her while his lean hips pressed her deeper into the soft earth. Lindsay found

her body instinctively arching against Jason's, as his lips
found the pulse in her throat.

His lean fingers moved softly, gently pushing her offend-
ing sweater upward, and she felt the thin bra fall aside.
She was acutely aware of the feel of his chest against her
naked skin, and of the excitement and pleasure that shot
through her at the pure sensation of it. She felt an ache
deep within, a desire to be even closer to Jason, and threw
her arms around his dark body to grasp him to her. She
could feel his strong muscles ripple under her fingers.

She gasped with unexpected pleasure as she felt his lips
move down to her breasts to kiss them, causing the nipples
to swell and harden in her excitement. She had never felt
this way in her life and only wanted this feeling to continue. If this was the way Jason had planned on punishing
her, then she would accept it. No, she *wanted* it with all
her heart and soul.

The pine needles pressed into her back as Jason lay
above her, making love to her, each of them growing short
of breath. Lindsay's breathing grew more ragged as she
pressed her lips against Jason's chest, her hands around his
neck holding him close. She heard him gasp, and he
grabbed her arms and held them tightly to his heaving
chest. His lips moved upward from the fire they were
trailing across her breasts, and buried themselves once
more in her neck. He held her strongly and motionlessly,
moving slowly and purposefully but preventing her from
further movement. Her fingers entwined themselves in the
dark hair of his chest. As Lindsay was trying to catch her
own breath, she felt Jason's dark head shake slightly, and
caught the words murmured against her throat.

"No . . . no, damn it!" He raised his head and stared
into Lindsay's bewildered and stormy eyes with a bleak
look. He lay there, holding her still and just stared at her,
his look becoming more composed and cool. He took in a
deep breath and released her, moving to sit upright at her
side. He ran a shaky hand through his hair and stared at
the lake, his breathing still quick.

Lindsay lay there, hurt and frustrated, not understanding Jason's sudden withdrawal. She reached up and placed a shaking hand on his bare arm, her voice quivering with her hurt and bewilderment. "Why, Jason? Why are you doing this to me? Did you plan this all along?" Her voice stopped, unable to continue, tears brimming in her eyes.

Gently, he adjusted her clothing, and forced himself to look at her. His eyes were dark and stormy, as if he were at a loss to understand something. Then the look was gone, veiled by his dark lashes. His face became inscrutable, like the Jason of old, blank and unreadable.

Sitting there, he looked like the Indian he was, acting as if nothing at all had happened between them, yet Lindsay knew that was not so. Something *had* happened and that something had changed everything between Jason and herself, even if he wouldn't admit it. She felt hurt and angry and hated him for what he had done. She hated him! She had allowed herself to be exposed to emotions that no one else in the world had ever extracted from her. She had willingly let herself go, drawn by the intensity and fire of this dark man, drawn along with him on that sea of passion, wanting to match him emotion for emotion, sensation for sensation, to learn, to accept anything he wanted to teach her. And he had abruptly broken it off, unfeelingly, casually.

He sat for a long time, staring out over the lake, frowning. Lindsay drew upon her small reserve of pride and sat up, drawing her legs up to her chest, her lips bruised and swollen from the expertise of Jason Mainwaring. She now knew what the saying "You look like you've just been kissed" meant, and bitterly resented it. She was ashamed of her uninhibited response to this man, but she was just as determined not to ever allow him to see that.

"There are too many years between us, Lindsay. I respect your father's friendship too much to disregard it like that. And my father loves you too much. Times have changed, Lindsay. You have your whole life ahead of you and shouldn't become involved with me."

The hurt came through her voice as she asked in a

145

small voice, "And what about my feelings, Jason? You've taken everyone else's into account—yours, my father's, and your father's. Did you ever stop to ask what my feelings were about what just happened?"

He looked at her squarely and answered coldly, "You're too inexperienced to know what your feelings are. Hell, you came up here to find out what you wanted to do with your life. Do you think I'm going to allow a brief experiment on both our parts to interfere with that? You're just starting to find out what you want and I'm not going to be the one to start messing around with your emotions. You already thought you were madly in love, and you were wrong. You still haven't had the chance to find out that sex is not love, Lindsay, and whether you like it or not, I'd prefer not to be the one to teach you."

She stared at him, refusing to flinch at his hurtful words, yet knowing that he was tearing her heart apart by saying them. She forced a shrug and said tightly, "I really learned one thing from this afternoon's experience, Jason, and I really should thank you for it."

He looked at her, one dark eyebrow arched, and asked quietly, "What's that, Lindsay?"

She gave him a saccharine smile and answered, standing up and brushing off her still-wet jeans, "I think I hate you more than anyone in the whole world. That's what you taught me this afternoon, Jason!" She turned her back on him and started to walk back toward the house. She knew that she had spoken only in pride. Jason had taught her something all right, she thought bitterly. Jason had taught her that she loved him more than she had ever thought possible. Just when she had been willing to give him anything he would have asked for, he had coldly rejected her. Thank goodness she had never whispered the words that had come to her lips just as he had pulled away from her. Those damning words that now he would never know and never hear—*I love you. I love you, Jason.* She shivered in her wet clothes, and walked purposely toward Jason's car. She could wait until she reached her cabin to change.

She was standing by the rider's side of the car, her hand

on the door, when Jason finally walked up from the lake. He was carrying his sweater in one hand and stopped in front of her.

"If you think I'm taking you home in those sopping clothes, you're wrong. And get that look off your face. I have a clothes dryer inside that'll dry them in fifteen minutes. You need some brandy anyway. I know I do. And Lindsay, I'm not going to apologize for this afternoon. I remember apologizing once for kissing you. I never apologize the second time. You were warned about provoking me. This time you paid the price." His eyes lit momentarily with a slight touch of humor.

She glared at him. "You egotist!" Her lips were held together in a stiff line and she felt her body start to shiver again from the cold. He grabbed her by the arm and marched her inside the warm house and up the spiral staircase.

"Go into the bedroom and take off everything. And don't look at me that way. I'm merely trying to prevent you from catching pneumonia! You'll find a terry cloth robe on the back of the door. You can satisfy your modesty and my good intentions by wearing that while I throw those clothes into the dryer. When you come out, you'll find a large glass of brandy sitting by the fireplace. Sit on a pillow next to the fireplace and drink it. The fire'll take off the chill."

Lindsay stamped into Jason's bedroom, annoyed at his orders. She was cold and wet and now she felt worse than she had early that morning. She must really be coming down with a cold and the quicker she got into warm clothes and drank that brandy, the better off she'd be. And the sooner he'd take her home! She didn't think she could bear to be around him much longer.

She tore off her clothes, noting that her skin was icy cold, and throwing on his bathrobe, tossed the wet clothes into his waiting arms. He disappeared downstairs and she sat down and drank the brandy, rubbing her arms with shaking hands, trying to get the circulation going again.

She watched Jason come up the stairs again and march

into the bedroom, to reappear in moments wearing a different and certainly much drier set of clothes. For a brief moment, as he stood there looking at her, observing that she had finished the brandy, she felt her heart jump violently again. He was still potently attractive in his corded cream pants and black sweater, and she was once again reminded of how those tight muscles had felt under her hands, of the silky feel of the black hairs on his lean chest, of his hard mouth on hers, demanding and possessive.

She avoided his piercing gaze as she finished the brandy, aware of her nakedness beneath his robe, her skin still radiating heat from the memory of his hands and lips. She had to get out of here while she could still think clearly. His nearness was starting to cloud her thoughts, or was it the effect of the brandy on her empty stomach?

"Jason, I want to go home now." Her voice was husky and quiet.

He gazed down at her, his eyes drawn to her forefinger that was unconsciously fingering the rim of the brandy snifter, evidence of her nervousness. He shook his head and answered with authority, his lips tight in controlled vexation. "You've got to get something hot into you first. That brandy will only warm you temporarily. I'll put a can of soup on. We could both use it right now."

She shook her head with determination. The last thing she needed at this moment was to sit and eat with Jason, acting as if nothing had happened. She stared at his hand, noting the fine black hairs and remembering his touch as he reached down and quickly poured her one more brandy. She now knew all too well the power that that lean hand had and the fiery response it could evoke in her.

"No, I don't want soup and I don't want any more brandy. I'm fine. I just want my clothes, please." She was amazed at how firm and cool her voice sounded. She was a bundle of nerves inside, yet she was still able to maintain a facade of civility and calm. She felt as if that bubble of hysteria caught in her throat would burst at any moment. She forced her eyes to meet his confused ones and stared at his face without blinking.

148

He frowned and took a deep breath, gesturing with his hands in a placating manner. "All right, if that's what you want, but I think you're rushing it. Your hair is still damp even if your clothes have dried by now." He smiled slightly as he said, "But I do make a mean can of soup!"

He turned and started down the staircase. He was just at the bottom of the stairs when the doorbell rang. Lindsay glanced down at her state of undress. Great! Now what? This was all she needed—someone walking in and finding her here like this. She glanced around and decided that Jason's bedroom was the last place she should go. Her curiosity got the better of her, and she softly tread toward the top of the staircase, the sounds of her bare feet muffled by the deep, soft shag rug. As she stood there listening, the thought ran through her head that at any other time the situation would have been humorous. She had played the role of eavesdropper once before. She heard Jason's deep voice and then the breathless murmur that she remembered all too well.

"Darling, I tried to reach you all day by phone and couldn't so I came right over. Where on earth have you been? You do remember that we're invited to Edward and Sylvia's for dinner tonight?"

Lindsay bit her bottom lip and quietly stepped down a few more steps. She wasn't usually nosy but something drove her on. Finally she saw Jason and Marcia standing in the foyer, the sunlight shining through the glass surrounding the door to reflect brilliantly off the blond cap of Marcia's hair. As usual she was dressed to perfection and Lindsay found herself wondering if there was ever a time that Marcia didn't have every hair in place. Her eyes had turned green, jealous lights directed at the tiny blonde who stood there, her arms wrapped around Jason's neck.

Jason stood, tall and dark, his head held to one side as he smiled down at Marcia, his hands resting lightly on her slim waist. "Of course I remember," he said. "Your father reminded me the other day when I was with him. What's the problem?" His dark gaze shifted for a moment to the staircase and Lindsay stepped back. Had Jason sensed that she was standing there, or was he afraid that Marcia would see her and demand to know why she was there?

A slightly devilish smile hovered at his firm lips as he turned his devastating gaze back to Marcia. He pulled her closer to him and Lindsay scowled, furious at the ease with which he could turn his attention from one female to another. How dare he! Her attention was directed once again to Marcia as she heard her reply, her eyes looking up into Jason's face with adoration.

"Well, Daddy forgot to tell you that it's black tie. Oh, Jason, don't look like that. You'd think you were ready to go to the hangman! You look so attractive when you dress up and I'm so proud of you. Please? For me?"

Sure, Lindsay thought, proud to be seen with him. I bet they make a beautiful pair, the envy of everyone around them. She probably leads him around the room, showing him off like some grand prize she's won! Well, I don't have to sit here and listen to any more of this delightful exchange. I am at this moment feeling quite *de trop!* She froze at Jason's words and found herself shaking as her slim hand found the rail.

"Marcia darling, I would do anything for the woman I love, anything. If you say it's black tie, than for once I guess I can go without grumbling." With that he drew her into his arms and planted a firm kiss on her mouth. Furious, Lindsay walked on trembling legs down the stairs, almost tripping over Jason's bathrobe in the process.

At her sudden appearance, Marcia's eyes widened and that sudden look of jealousy and hatred toward Lindsay showed for a brief moment. Jason released her slowly, one dark eyebrow raised, a slight smile of amusement playing at the corner of his lips. Lindsay glared at his dark face, now expressionless, and said in a tight voice, "If you both will pardon the interruption, I'll go get my clothes now." She held her head high as she brushed past the two of them and darted a fiery glance at Jason as she passed.

She thought she heard Jason chuckle slightly as she entered the den and heard Marcia's quick demand for an explanation. Let him sort that one out, she thought with satisfaction. Walking over to the dryer, Lindsay quickly drew out her jeans and sweater. With a sigh of relief she noted that they were warm and dry. Her thin bra and panties slipped from her hand as she laid the bundle on top of the dryer and swiftly removed the robe. Her hands trembled as she hooked her bra, remembering suddenly how quickly it had come undone under Jason's smooth fingers. She closed her eyes tightly and swallowed. Lord, how had she ever let this happen. She had never meant to fall in love with Jason, and now she knew that he would never love her. She had heard him admit to Marcia a few moments ago that he loved *her*. She must never let Jason know how she really felt about him. He thought her an impulsive child, and obviously wanted a sophisticated beauty like Marcia at his side. She quickly threw on the remainder of her clothes and tied her sneakers. Even they had dried in the clothes dryer.

Walking out into the front of the house, she saw Marcia standing in the hallway, waiting for her, her eyes brittle and sharp despite the cool smile directed at Lindsay. Jason was in the study on the phone, ruffling through some blueprints on his desk, his voice impatient, his quick anger directed at the person on the other end of the line. It was obvious that he was talking to one of his workmen.

Marcia looked at Lindsay and said coolly, "Jason explained the mishap. You can understand my dismay at seeing you wearing his bathrobe. It can be most disconcerting to a woman to find a partially undressed girl in her fiancé's house, even though you are cousins. I can't imagine what got into Jason's mind to take you out in that canoe of his. I should think it most uncomfortable to sit in and, as you found out the hard way, it's far too unsafe for an inexperienced girl. Oh, well, the incident won't repeat itself, will it, Lindsay?" She stared intently into Lindsay's blue-green eyes, her own blue eyes icy.

Lindsay felt close to the breaking point and found that she had no desire to even converse with this coldly calculating woman. She turned toward the study door and said sharply, "Believe me, it'll never happen again. Not if I have anything to say about it!" There, let Marcia think about that remark for a while. "How long will Jason be on the phone? I want to get home." She glanced at Marcia, who was still summing her up with that cool expression.

"Oh, I imagine for quite a while. The call came in while you were dressing, but don't let that worry you. I was just leaving and I'll be more than happy to take you to your cabin, Lindsay."

I'll bet you will, thought Lindsay. She can't wait to get me out of Jason's hair. She glanced one more time into the study and saw the frown of concentration on Jason's face. She chewed her lip and turned to face Marcia.

"Thanks, I'll take you up on that offer. I want to get home and take a shower and wash my hair. That water was like ice." She walked past Marcia and out the door. If Marcia expected her to be upset that Jason couldn't take her home, she was in for a disappointment. She stepped into the front seat and tried to relax, waiting for Marcia to tell Jason where they were going. But Marcia was right behind her and immediately set the car in motion.

Lindsay sat quietly, not feeling like talking. Certainly Marcia and she had nothing in common—except their love for Jason Mainwaring, she thought with a slight pain in her chest. Jason had made that very clear in the foyer. He preferred and wanted Marcia. He didn't consider Lindsay old enough to know what she wanted.

She closed her eyes tightly; her chest hurt and so did every muscle in her body. Her head was throbbing and she couldn't swallow because of the tightness in her throat. What a time for a cold, she thought.

"You know, Lindsay, we haven't really had a chance to get to know each other. We should really spend the time to have an old-fashioned, girl-to-girl talk, don't you think?" Marcia's brittle smile seemed out of place in the smooth beauty of her face.

Lindsay looked out the window and answered, "Well, I don't think I'll be here that long, Marcia. I only came up to take a small vacation and to paint. Didn't Jason tell you that?" She looked at Marcia questioningly.

"Well, actually Jason has been rather reluctant to discuss you. I assumed there was some deep family secret that he didn't want to divulge. You have no idea how secretive that man can be at times. But since you and I will be part of the family once Jason and I are married, perhaps you can tell me more about yourself. Really, I'm most interested in getting to know you better."

I'll just bet you are, Lindsay thought as she took in the innocent look in Marcia's eyes.

"Actually, there is no deep, dark secret, Marcia," she said, "Although I'm sure that most families have them. Jason and I only met a couple times when we were young—well, I think I remember Jason being around when I was only about five or so, just a baby. He was always the older, grown-up, but treated me like anyone else would his age. There's not anything I can tell you. Our families are extremely close and have remained that way over these many years, even though Jason has been away."

"And how would you define your relationship with Jason now, Lindsay?" Marcia asked sharply.

Lindsay thought desperately, her mind clouded by the effects of the brandy that was just now taking effect. She drew in a breath and slowly released it and answered quietly, "Exactly as you see it, Marcia. There *is* no relationship to speak of. There are too many years between us and I hardly know the Jason I see now, just as he doesn't recognize me as the young child he carried on his shoulders. We have only the past between us, and Jason's compassionate feeling for me as the little cousin he still looks out for—like a big brother. He's very kind that way, or hadn't you noticed? And me, well, I am grateful for that kindness." She stared straight ahead. It's all I'll ever receive from Jason, she thought.

Marcia drove quickly, her lips pursed as if she was thinking about Lindsay's explanation. She raised an eyebrow and said, "How old are you now, Lindsay? You don't look more than about sixteen or seventeen."

Lindsay looked down and smiled. She knew that Marcia

had no idea she had been the "toast of Washington." But that was over now.

"I'm old enough, Marcia. I'm surprised at you. It's sacrilege for one woman to reveal her age to another." She chuckled at the surprised expression on Marcia's carefully made-up face.

The car came to an abrupt halt and Lindsay realized that they had reached the cabin. She dragged herself wearily out of the car and turned to thank Marcia for driving her over. Marcia sat straight, her eyes ahead, obviously upset over something. Somehow it pleased Lindsay that Marcia could be troubled.

"Thanks for the ride, Marcia," she called, "I'd invite you in for some coffee but I'm tired and want that shower. Besides, I'm sure you'll want to hurry back to Jason. Thank him for me for the ride in the canoe and for the use of the bathrobe. Tell him I don't plan on repeating the experience in the future!" She laughed silently to herself and stepped back as Marcia tore out of the driveway. She was certain Jason was in for an earful when Marcia reached his house.

Turning, Lindsay walked up the stairs, wanting only to shower and slip into bed.

Her arms ached as she dried her body, now chilly and shaking. She forced herself to use the blow-dryer to dry her hair, realizing that she couldn't go to bed with a wet head, and took a couple of aspirin to try and ease the throbbing ache in her head and back. Lethargically, she slipped the long flannel nightgown over her head and climbed into bed and under the warm comforter. Even this action seemed to sap her of strength and she couldn't seem to shake the chills that came over her, despite the thick covers over her. She lifted a hand to her forehead and felt the penetrating heat flow through to her hand and knew that she was running a fever as well as chills. Perhaps the aspirin would help. She buried her aching head into the soft pillows and fell into a fitful sleep.

Chapter Eleven

Lindsay awoke with a start and glanced at the dark bedroom. With a soft groan she lifted the bedside clock and noted that she had been asleep for a good six hours. It was now ten o'clock at night and as she sat up, rubbing her stiff neck, she felt as if she had slept the sleep of the dead.

At least she felt a little better as she sniffed and reached for a tissue to blow her nose. Her fever seemed to have subsided but her throat ached more than before. She lay in the soft bed, trying to force her lethargic mind to function. Should she try to eat something, or just take some more aspirin and go back to bed and try to sleep this blasted cold off? If she were home in her father's house, she would have had all kinds of cold remedies and would have felt the luxury of being waited on and catered to. But she wasn't home and she would just have to forget any pampering from Emerson or her father.

Her father! She jumped out of bed and quickly wrapped her bathrobe around her as she slipped her feet into her slippers. She had meant to phone him this morning before Jason had arrived and taken her to his house.

As she made her way cautiously into the living room, she groped for the table and lit the lamp. Reaching down, she picked up the receiver and with fumbling fingers placed a call to her father. She pulled a chair under her as she waited anxiously for the phone at the other end to be answered. She sneezed and found another tissue in her pocket just as she heard that familiar gruff voice that she loved so much.

"Yes? Who's calling, please." He sounded rushed and she wondered if she had interrupted a late meeting in his study.

"Dad, it's me. Am I interrupting anything?" Her voice sounded like the croak of a bullfrog and she swallowed, cursing herself for not having drunk something before she had called to wet her parched throat.

"What's wrong with you? You sound like you're sick!" her father growled.

Lindsay smiled to herself, imagining her father's full white eyebrows scowling in censure. "I just have a small head cold, that's all. I'm perfectly all right, Dad. How are you?"

"I'm fine. Miss you, though. How's the painting coming along? Have you finally relaxed enough to enjoy yourself?"

With a wry smile, she thought: Oh, yes, Dad, I just developed a broken heart along with this damn cold, that's all. Otherwise, everything's just fine. Instead, she deliberately cleared her throat and forced a bit of lightness into her voice.

"It's been everything I had hoped for and more. I think I've found something that I really am good at, Dad. Besides being decorative, that is," she added drily. "I love painting, and I think I might go on to a good school when I come home. What do you think?" She tried to sound casual, praying that he wouldn't bring up Jason's name. She didn't think she could manage to fool her father for long if he questioned her about Jason. He knew her emotions and feelings as well as she did and had always been able to tell when she was upset about something. He had a second sense about his daughter that was only secondary to his love for her.

"Well, honey, if that's what you really want, than I'm

all for it. When are you coming home?" His deep voice softened at the question.

She shut her eyes and tried to sound calm. If she had had her way, she would have stayed up here in Vermont with Jason for the rest of her life, if he had really wanted her. But then, he didn't want her. She must leave here as soon as she could. She had found out what she wanted for herself, perhaps more than she had bargained for. She had found love—an unrequited love—and she must push it into the deeper recesses of her mind and try to go on with her life.

"I think in one more week or so," she answered. "I'm almost finished with the fall scenes, and there's nothing to keep me here once the leaves fall. I miss you, Dad." A note of sadness reached out to him across the miles and he cleared his throat.

"Are you certain that you're all right, honey? Where are you calling me from, Jason's?"

"No! That is, Jason had a phone put in the cabin so I could speak to you whenever I wanted to. Actually, I think he got tired of having to drive all the way over here to take me to his house to use a phone. He's a busy man and I think my being here is interrupting him. He thinks I'm a pain in the neck, I'm sure."

"It does sound as if you two are having some difficulties."

She answered sarcastically, "Yes, we seem to fight the moment we get together. I can't be in the same room with him for over one minute then war breaks out. He's totally unrealistic and an egotist. I can't wait to leave here. I'll be eternally grateful for the day when I won't have to see him again!"

"Yes, I seem to have heard you say that before about Jason. Can't quite say that I ever remember any man striking you quite as strongly as Jason has. He is a quietly willful man, but I've always found him to be reasonable about most things."

"He's a tyrant! You just remember him as a young man. He's changed, Father. I'm seeing him as he really is.

I don't like him, I'm sorry." Her voice faltered and she reached for her handkerchief once again.

"*Hmm*, interesting isn't it? You see him as the man and I see him as the boy he once was. It couldn't be that you have this extremely strong dislike for Jason because he's one man you can't manipulate, could it, Lindsay Sheffield?" Her father sounded amused and Lindsay was angered by his shrewdness.

"No!" she hotly denied. "And what do you mean by insinuating that I would try and manipulate Jason? An angel from heaven on high couldn't wrap Jason Mainwaring around her delicate finger. He's untouchable and unapproachable. And I couldn't care less about him. Subject closed!"

"Well, you always have been able to have any man you wanted, my dear, and Jason isn't exactly the bending type. It would take quite a woman to bring him down on his knees, I know that much. He's proud but has great principles, my dear, and I think you do him a discredit to think otherwise."

"Oh, Dad, I'm not going to argue with you about him. We both feel entirely different about him. I'm going to get some warm milk and go to bed. You sleep well and I'll call you just before I come home, okay?" She suddenly found her head going around in circles and wondered if the conversation about Jason had precipitated it or the sudden fit of coughing that she felt coming on.

"Good night, sweetheart. Get rid of that cold quickly. If you can attack this cold as quickly as you attack Jason, you'll get it out of your system soon." He chuckled softly and she shook her tired head, knowing that her father would insist on having the last word about Jason.

She hung up the phone and turned off the light. Suddenly a paroxysm of coughing hit her and it took her a few painful moments to recover. She stood, breathless and shaking, and moved with wobbling steps toward the bathroom. Once again she felt feverish and her lungs ached from the coughing. She reached into the medicine closet and took two more aspirins. Looking up into the mirror, she saw her flushed cheeks and the dull look in her eyes. Her lips and throat were dry, and after she washed her face with cool water and brushed her teeth quickly, Lindsay turned and slowly moved toward the bed, climbing under the covers.

She soon found that she couldn't lie flat or she would start coughing again, so she finally propped her pillows up and fell into a fitful sleep in a half-sitting position.

The next three days followed almost the same pattern. Lindsay felt worse each day and attributed it to a bout of the flu and not just the simple cold that she had at first thought. She tried to force down some toast and tea on occasion, but soon gave up trying to eat. She suffered extremes of fever and then shaking chills, and ached in every part of her body. She had lost weight and now her face was deathly pale and deep blue circles surrounded her eyes. All she wanted to do was to stay in bed under the covers.

She would fall into periods of deep sleep. She thought at times that she heard the ringing of the telephone, but each time she forced herself out of her bed to answer it, she found no one on the line. At times she thought her ears were playing tricks on her and she could swear that she heard music playing somewhere. She soon gave up answering the phone after four occasions when she heard the ringing and decided that the head cold was causing the noises. Besides, at that point, feeling as badly as she did, she didn't care anymore.

On the third day she debated whether or not to call Jason and ask him to obtain a prescription for some cold preparation for her. But at the last minute, she hung up the phone, determined not to allow him to enter her life and take over again. She would see this bout of flu through herself. What could a doctor do for her anyway except tell her to rest, take two aspirin, and drink plenty of fluids? Her cough had gotten worse and she was reduced to staying in bed all day, only getting up to drink canned juices and to shower.

She lost track of time and slept off and on, grateful that

159

the coughing spells had subsided, even though her chest had grown tight and painful. Once again she thought she heard the ring of the phone and she turned over fitfully, waiting for the noise to go away. She fell asleep again and thought she heard Jason's voice calling to her, a cool, firm hand pressed on her hot forehead. She tried to push the hand away. It was disturbing her sleep and all she wanted to do was sleep. She thought she heard her own voice protesting this violation in a murmur, but the persistent voice of Jason and then of another male voice kept awaking her.

She dreamed that Jason was bending over her, lifting her in his arms, forcing cool water down her throat. Yet the water tasted odd, almost bitter. She was so parched that she drank thirstily, and then fell asleep again.

The dreams came and went and Jason was constantly in them, ordering her about, telling her what to do. She was amazed to find an odd comfort in his commands. The ache in her chest lessened and she felt less feverish and deduced that the sleep must have helped her and time had finally started to heal her. Her head throbbed and she tried to rouse herself from her dreams and return to reality.

She opened her eyes and noted the lamp lit on a table on the far side of the room. She squinted at it. She must still be dreaming. She had never lit that lamp. She sighed and reached a shaking hand up to feel her forehead. It still felt hot, but for some reason she no longer had the head cold or the sore throat. Lindsay tried to stretch her tired legs and found them weak.

Shaking her head, she determinedly threw the covers aside and tried to sit up. Immediately the room started spinning. She held a hand to the bedside and reached up and held her whirling head with the other. She was weaker than she had realized.

Stepping out of bed, she ignored her slippers and robe. She looked for them briefly but couldn't remember where she had put them. With a puzzled frown, she started to walk toward the bathroom on legs that felt like jelly. Suddenly she was stopped in her tracks by a sharp command from an all too familiar voice.

"And where in hell do you think you're going, might I ask? Get back in bed right now or I'll carry you there myself." Jason stood in the doorway, leaning lazily against the door jamb, one hand raised nonchalantly over his head, the other resting on his hip. What was more disturbing than anything was the fact that he was wearing his terry cloth bathrobe—and only that. His bare legs beneath it testified to that. His angry eyes darted black sparks at her and his lips were set in a tight line. The dark scowl on his angular face made him look even more terrifying to Lindsay.

She stood there, unbelieving. She was still asleep. How could Jason be here in her bedroom, dressed like that? A sudden chill shook her and she found that she had suddenly felt sick and couldn't move toward the bed. Her legs could just about hold her up, she couldn't take her widened eyes off Jason and stood mutely as he marched across the room and swept her up into his arms as if she were a child. He walked across the room and laid her gently on the large bed, tucking the covers firmly around her slight body.

He stood tall, glaring grimly down at her bewildered eyes, taking in the gauntness of her tiny body beneath the covers in the large bed. He watched as her lips tried to form words.

Lindsay couldn't believe this. She knew now that she was no longer asleep. She felt Jason's steellike hands holding her body close to his and she had felt the firm muscles of his chest ripple beneath her slim hands as she had instinctively placed them against him when he had swept her up into his arms. He was here in the cabin. He was also undressed and looked as if he had been sleeping. She remembered suddenly that he had a bedroom here also. But what was he doing here and why hadn't she heard him come over? How long had he been here?

"Jason, what are you doing here? I don't understand . . ."

He interrupted her confused murmur and answered gently, "I've been staying here the last three days, Lindsay.

You've been very sick. You almost had penumonia on top
of the flu. We've been taking care of you and I must admit that if you hadn't started to come out of that fever by
this morning, Dr. Joyce would have admitted you to the
hospital."

Lindsay's eyes widened as she listened to his words. It
couldn't be. She shook her dark head in confusion. Certainly she had had a cold and hadn't felt well, but how
many days had she lost? The dreams she had had . . . she
remembered hearing the strange voices . . . Jason's . . .
another man's . . . this Dr. Joyce, perhaps?

"Jason, if you've been here for three days, then who—I
mean who took care of me and why can't I remember getting that sick?" Her heart beat furiously as she realized
that Jason had been here with her all that time. He had
bathed her and changed her nightgowns. She glanced
down at the gown she was now wearing and tried to think
back, but her mind and body were too weary. Certainly it
wasn't the same gown she had gone to bed in.

Closing her eyes, she lay back in the pillows and listened to the quiet timbre of Jason's voice as he continued.
There seemed a touch of amusement in his voice, or perhaps her mind was now working overtime and she was just
imagining it.

"I can see that you're worried over the proprieties. Just
to set the record straight, I hired a nurse to work the
morning and afternoon shifts. She gave you the tender loving care that you needed."

She interrupted suddenly. "Then why did you stay here
with me if I had a nurse taking care of me?"

He grinned and said in a very clear and logical tone, as
if he were explaining to a child, "You had a very high fever and the nurse couldn't get fluids down you. Plus, you
wouldn't take your medicine." His eyes lifted to the ceiling
over her head as he almost piously continued. "It seems I
was the only one who could get you to take that medicine.
You tend to be a bit temperamental, Lindsay, and I guess
you just needed a stronger hand than the nurse could
provide." His sparkling eyes danced over her.

Her lips compressed as she said tightly, "And I just bet you enjoyed every moment of it, didn't you, bullying me around and once again taking over and telling me what to do! And there I was, defenseless against you. I bet the nurse thought the world of you, being able to handle me so easily!"

He chuckled softly, "Oh, come on, Lindsay. You've never been defenseless against anyone in your whole life. You just weren't very compliant during that brief period, that's all."

"And just how did that brief period start? I thought I was just fine taking care of myself. I never called you and asked for your expert and unsolicited opinion. What made you come over?" she asked defiantly.

"I phoned you several times but you never answered the phone. It's quite simple after that. I got worried and came over. By that time you were in the bedroom and out like a light. You were as hot as hell and shaking with chills and you didn't respond to me at all. I heard that cough and got on the phone and called Dr. Joyce. He's a family friend. He made a quick diagnosis of flu and possible pneumonia. We were afraid to move you because of the fever, so he agreed to allow a private duty nurse to take over your care as long as your condition didn't deteriorate. If the antibiotics didn't bring that fever down in two days, he was going to admit you to the nearest hospital. The fever started dropping early this morning and things started looking up. Dr. Joyce said you'd be coming around by this afternoon. It looks as if he was right. You seem to be the same willful, obstinate child that you always were!" His face looked dark as the shadows in the room played off his angular cheeks, but Lindsay could swear that under the light play of Jason's words there was an undertone of deep concern. Certainly, she rationalized, he wouldn't have stayed if he hadn't been concerned.

"So what now, Oh Great Healer? Can I get out of bed and go to the bathroom and take a bath and brush my teeth, or do I have to wait for my angel in her white uniform to give me a bed bath?"

163

"I can see you're recovering faster than we expected. Well, let's see. I see no reason why you can't take a quick bath—after *I* fill the tub and get the bathroom warm. I think I know by now where your fresh nightgowns are. They're quite quaint, by the way, and since your bed was changed this afternoon I can't see why you shouldn't get freshened up." His eyes twinkled as he took in the set of Lindsay's lips as she looked up quickly as his words registered.

"And how was my bed changed, Jason? Did they roll me from one side to the other, just like they do the really sick patients in the hospitals?" she asked irritably.

"Oh, no. We didn't fool with any of that nonsense here. We did it the easy way."

"We?" she said questioningly.

"Yes, *we*. I swept you up in my arms, blanket and all, and sat with you in my lap while the nurse quickly changed the bed. It's amazing how much you look and feel like an angelic child when you're quiet and sleeping. You'd never know . . ."

"Know what?" she demanded, furious that she had been held in Jason's arms, unaware of his closeness, and now aware of an ache deep within her, an ache from the knowledge that she would never again feel this man's arms, that he belonged to another woman. She felt tears well suddenly behind her eyes and quickly glanced away from him. Somehow this was all too civilized—the two of them sitting in her bedroom, both undressed and holding a conversation. With all her heart she wanted him to hold her in his arms now, to press her head against his chest so that she could feel the strong beat of his heart, to feel the hard pressure of his demanding lips, and to surrender to that demand. She dragged her thoughts away from such fantasies and shrugged slightly.

"Never mind. How about that bath, Jason? I really could use it. My back is one huge ache from lying here."

"Fine. You're wearing yourself out by talking anyway. A quick bath and back to bed, young lady. I expect to see some sparkle back in those eyes tomorrow." He turned and started for the bathroom, halting momentarily as he heard her softly spoken words.

"Jason? Thank you for putting up with me. I guess I must have been a pain in the neck for everyone." She glanced down at the covers, fingering the threads. "Thanks for caring . . ."

He stood there quietly, taking in her forlorn look and hunched shoulders. After a few moments he answered so softly that she wasn't certain she had heard him.

"I care."

Lindsay's eyes darted swiftly upward but he was entering the bathroom and closing the door. She shut her tired eyes and pulled the covers up around her chin.

Jason was as good as his word. He filled the old tub with hot water and mounds of sweet-smelling suds.

Lindsay brushed her hair and coiled it up on top of her head, and after brushing her teeth, slipped into the comforting tub. The water came up under her chin and as she lay in it drowsily until the aches finally began to leave her body. She almost fell asleep when she heard a sharp rap on the door. Her eyes opened quickly and she grabbed the large, fluffy bathsheet that Jason had laid next to her clean gown.

"Let's go, Lindsay," he called. "Back to bed. It's time for your medicine. Are you all right?"

His voice demanded an answer and she yelled through the wooden door, "I'm okay. I'll be right out."

She quickly dried herself off and dusted her now warm body with scented powder. Donning her nightgown, slippers, and robe, she quickly opened the door and darted across the room to hop into the bed, throwing her robe across the bottom of the bed as she pulled the comforter up to her chin. Just as she was propping the pillows behind her back, the door opened and Jason, now dressed in black pants and a black pullover turtleneck sweater, entered carrying a bowl of steaming soup. Once again Lindsay found herself thinking how much Jason resembled a large black panther as he crossed the room in long, powerful strides. With his rippling muscles he could reach out and hold his prey helpless. She knew that that was how Jason made her feel each time she was with him and how she would always feel about him. Her body reacted to him without her consent, but then, there was nothing civilized about Jason Mainwaring, especially when his own feelings and emotions were aroused. She had learned that the hard way.

He handled the bowl with ease and sat down carefully on the edge of the bed, placing a towel over her front. The soup smelled delicious and for the first time in a week Lindsay realized that she was really hungry. She reached greedily for the spoon and quickly tasted the hot soup, smiling with pleasure.

"I told you I make a mean pot of soup. If you had stayed for it you might not have gotten into this mess. At least I could have taken you home dry and warm!" She noted the hint of humor in his deep voice.

She wrinkled her nose and answered drily, "You had other things on your mind when I left. Besides, one of those things drove me home, remember?" Her eyes lifted from the spoon to gaze into his own black ones.

"Ah yes. You escaped my clutches with the help of the good witch."

"It was kind of her to offer to drive me home. But then, I don't think she really approved of my attire when she saw me," Lindsay retorted.

"No, I can honestly say that she did not approve," Jason admitted calmly.

Jason obviously wasn't in the mood to tell Lindsay what had happened when Marcia had driven back to his home. She finished the soup and handed him the bowl. She had to admit she did feel much better.

Her eyes were drooping. Jason picked up a bottle on the nightstand, shook out two pink pills, and held them out to her.

"Here, I think you can start to take these by mouth now. It was a lot harder crushing them and forcing you to swallow them in water." He smiled grimly as she took the glass of water and gulped down the pills. They tasted bitter.

"How much longer do I have to take this stuff? It's awful!"

"Another week, but once you start eating something, the bitter taste will disappear. You can get up tomorrow if you want and lie on the couch in the living room. I'll make you a fire before I leave."

Her heart stopped. Of course Jason couldn't stay here anymore. He had work to do and she was certain Marcia was furious that he had elected to stay at the cabin in the first place. He must be anxious to get her out of his hair. She sighed and nodded.

"Yes, of course. Does the nurse still have to stay here with me? I feel much better, Jason, and I don't need nursing care anymore, honestly I don't." She didn't want someone hovering over her. She wanted to be left alone. She had planned on leaving Vermont and getting away from Jason and the pain that developed every time she thought of him married to Marcia. She had told her father that she would be coming home soon.

"We'll see how you feel in the morning. Now go to sleep. If you need anything, I'll be in my room. Just yell and I'll hear you. I'm a light sleeper. All Indians are, remember?" He chuckled and she smiled wanly, feeling sleepy. She snuggled down into the bed and smiled contentedly as Jason pulled the covers up around her neck. She fell asleep before he left the room.

She was trying to catch her breath, gasping with the effort, but a thousand hands were drawing her back into the bed and forcing the covers around her, smothering her. A cold blast of air was causing her to shake violently. She tried to force the hands away but it was no use. Her body was growing weaker and weaker. She tried to scream for help, tried to say the name of the one person who would save her. With one last weak cry, she felt her body relax and succumb to the pulling hands.

"Lindsay! Lindsay! Wake up. It's all right! Wake up!"

Jason . . . It was Jason's voice and he was shaking her shoulders, forcing her awake. She had been dreaming. She reached up and drew a trembling hand across her forehead. She was freezing cold and couldn't stop herself from shaking.

"Lindsay, I'm here. Relax, relax. You had a nightmare and were calling out to me. You scared the hell out of me. You're ice cold!" He sat down on the bed and drew her to him, his firm hand holding her to him, fiercely rubbing her back and shoulders through the covers, trying to warm her. It was her undoing.

Throwing her arms around his neck, she cried, sobbing into his chest. "Please don't leave me yet, Jason. I'm so cold and I'm afraid to go back to sleep. I had a nightmare." She shivered, feeling frightened and alone, and she held onto Jason like a lifeline. Her grip tightened and his hands slid up to her arms, gently prying them loose.

"All right, Lindsay, all right." He sighed heavily. "I'll stay with you until you sleep, but I'm not going to play Sir Galahad and sit on the edge of this bed and freeze to death. Move over a bit and let me under those covers."

Unthinkingly, she quickly slid to the other side of the bed, her heart still pounding from fright. She was freezing, too, and only wanted the comfort of Jason's arms. As he slid under the covers, he propped one of the pillows under his head and turned on his side, facing her. His arm reached out and drew her slender, shivering body across the bed toward him.

"Try to stop shaking, Lindsay, and try to get warm. Take in a couple of deep breaths and relax. Maybe we'll both get some sleep."

But now she couldn't relax because it was all too apparent that Jason had been interrupted in the middle of his sleep and like the primitive that he was, he slept in the nude. He had kept on the terry cloth bathrobe but Lindsay was all too aware of the heat radiating from his long, hard body gently pressed against the length of her back and hips. One long arm firmly pressed her against him and she wondered at how comfortably her own smaller body fit

lame of Love

rm rested

. . . She felt the qu
. Heat radiated
cken against her forehead
eathed against her hair. He w
dsay . . . My God, what a
her and drew her full lips, this time n
or anger, but with a gentleness th
than any emotion he had ever sh
compliant, willing him to do wh
She could no longer fight her e

Jason lay still, holding he
nally with a deep sigh, he
tom a slight tap, and slid
side of the bed. Quick
the bed, he stood up
him. He stood with
see the expression
the most bewitc
not sure at th
what I want
make love
that it's
you. B
to do

ened a
  She knew s
this time. Even now, a
uation logically, her body wa
with an instinct of its own. She felt
him, wanting to feel the hardness of his che
breasts, with only the soft flannel her nightgown sep
them. Her own arm was draped across Jason's waist while
her other hand was caught between her breasts and his
chest. She could feel her fingers softly, involuntarily working their way into the fine hairs to feel his heartbeat
against her fingertips. She closed her eyes and lay there,
afraid to move, not wanting Jason to awaken, afraid of
what she might have started and yet almost delighting in

ickening
f his body
him as she
d.

re you doing to
rapped both arms
ainst his long body
ot in ruthless passion
at possessed her more
own toward her. She lay
atever he wished with her.
motions.

in his arms, not moving. Fi-
owered one arm, gave her bother away from him to the other
y sliding his muscular legs out of
drawing the bathrobe tightly around
his back to Lindsay, and she couldn't
on his dark face as he said, "You are
ing creature I have ever dealt with. I'm
s moment *how* to deal with you. I know
to do and I know what I should do. I want to
to you very badly, and believe me when I say
aking a tremendous effort to walk away from
t that, Lindsay, my angel, is just what I am going

ith determination, he walked in long strides to the
or and on out to his own room. Lindsay lay still, staring
t the ceiling with stricken eyes. He could have taken her
at that moment if he had chosen to, yet he had not. Why?
Jason? What stopped you, she wondered. It was clear to
her now that he didn't love her or he would have stayed
with her. She had been right, she thought bitterly. She
should have left immediately, before this had ever happened. She knew it was inevitable, that she and Jason
could not be near each other without eventually ending up
involved in some sort of physical relationship. They were
drawn together by pure animal magnetism. The time
would finally come when he would not be able to walk

170

away. That time had come for her this morning. She had given in to her responding emotions. But then, she was in love with Jason and that was the difference.

She sighed and got out of bed. She felt better physically but her emotions were in turmoil. She bathed and dressed, determined to put on the best face she could in front of Jason as possible.

Her legs still felt shaky, but she was hungry again. Walking into the kitchen, she saw Jason standing at the kitchen counter, pouring tea into a mug. He handed it to her without a word and stood watching the expression on her face.

She took in his clothes and looked over at the coffee on the stove. Gesturing with the mug of tea, she grimaced and asked sarcastically, "And exactly what do you intend for me to do with *this?*" A look of distaste covered her face, her eyes flashing.

His firm lips quivered at the corners. "Drink it, of course." His cool eyes watched her.

"You drink it! I want coffee, not weak tea! I feel just fine, thank you! And don't you dare tell me it's good for me. I know just what I want and I'm quite capable of making up my own mind!" She glared at him, daring him to contradict her.

"Are you certain you know what you want, Lindsay?"

She had opened her mouth to answer him when the phone rang. She looked at him and walked into the room to answer it. It was the nurse, asking if Mr. Mainwaring felt she should come in that day. Lindsay glanced into the kitchen and caught Jason's expression as she announced clearly, "Thank you, but that won't be necessary. The patient has recovered. Would you kindly sent your bill to the care of Miss Lindsay Sheffield, please? Mr. Mainwaring is not responsible for the professional services rendered to the patient. Yes, thank you, I appreciate all you have done. Good-bye." She hung up the receiver with a decisive click and marched into the kitchen.

"Did that make you happy?" Jason inquired casually.

"*Very* happy, thank you. I'm quite capable of taking care of myself. You keep forgetting that!"

"On the contrary, Lindsay, I'm very much aware of it. By the way, I've had the time in the last few days to look over your work. I hope you don't think I was being inquisitive, but I must say I was very impressed by what I saw, and lord knows, I'm no patron of the arts. You're good, Lindsay, damn good. My father was right when he said you should have been a painter. You've a natural talent. Have you come to any decision regarding your future and what you're going to do with it?" He took a sip of coffee and watched her intently.

Lindsay stared down at her mug of coffee. She would brazen it out. She had no future with Jason and she would never let him know how she felt.

"Yes, as a matter of fact. I'm going back to Washington. I want to see a few friends that I miss and I'm tired of the quiet up here. I miss the cultural centers. Now that the leaves have fallen, there's nothing left for me up here, is there? So I might as well go home and paint there. Who knows? I might end up having a one-woman show. Besides, I've done all I can up here. Jake isn't here and I take up too much of your life. You'll be getting married anyway, so we wouldn't see each other if I stayed. No, I'm going home to Washington. You . . . you *will* be getting married fairly soon, won't you?" Her heart broke when she asked the question, yet something forced her to ask it.

He stared quietly at her and answered musingly, "Yes, I guess I will. At least that's what I intend to do."

"Oh, well I'm sure things will go a lot smoother for you once I'm out from under your feet. I've interfered enough with Marcia and you. She's been very patient." It was amazing that she could utter such banalities with calm.

"Yes, I guess she has. Perhaps you're right, Lindsay. It might be the best thing for you to go home. You think you know what you want now, so go home and find it. Finish what you started. You ran away before. Now go back and be proud of what you've learned and done. Perhaps it would be best if you did try your hand at painting where it can best be appreciated. Put on your one-woman show and see how the public reacts to Lindsay Sheffield the artist, instead of Lindsay Sheffield, social butterfly. I think you'll be in for a very pleasant surprise, kitten. Give it a try."

"You think that's what I should really do, Jason?" she asked softly, tears brimming in her eyes.

"Yes, I do. If you don't try it, Lindsay, you'll always wonder whether or not you could have made it. I'd rather see you try it and fail then never give it the chance it deserves. Go home, Lindsay. Go home and really find out what is waiting for you."

Chapter Twelve

Lindsay stood before the floor-length mirror in her bedroom, staring intently at the figure reflected in shades of palest turquoise and jade green. She smiled wryly. One couldn't tell that behind that gracefully draped facade was a broken heart, shattered by three words that had been reverberating through her mind during the last five weeks: *Go home, Lindsay. Go home, Lindsay.* And so she had.

The week following the day Jason had casually spoken those words to her, she had quietly piled her things into the car, and driven back to Washington. This time she had broken the trip into several days, stopping at several motels to rest and recover from the illness. She had not seen Jason since that day but he had phoned her almost daily to check on her condition. She was grateful for the distance that the telephone placed between them. She found she could maintain a cool and polite front during their brief conversations. She knew he was busy completing one project and was just as content that his work prevented him from visiting her.

Five weeks . . . Christmas was just around the corner . . . and the goose was getting fat—wasn't that how the song went? But she realized she wasn't ready as she glanced at her too-slender figure. She had lost weight that she couldn't afford to lose. True, she had crammed every-

174

thing she could into her days, driving herself to finish the canvases, anything to keep Jason from her thoughts. Amazingly, her father had mentioned very little, if anything, of Jason. Her father was more concerned with the vehemence with which she drove herself, not stopping to eat, staying up late, and awakening early. But sleep brought memories of Jason and when she did sleep, it was fitfully.

But all the hard work had been worth it. G. Harold Linton, a well-known and popular art critic and owner of one of Washington's more elite galleries, had viewed her work with a critical eye. After he had looked over her paintings and sketches for what seemed an interminable length of time, he had judged that Lindsay indeed had a natural talent and that he would be honored to be the first to show her works to the Washington elite.

The ensuing weeks had been spent with Linton taking charge. He had studied each painting and sketch and had chosen a frame and matting for each one. His choices were perfect. At one point Lindsay, feeling great doubts about her ability, had frankly asked Mr. Linton if he was doing all this because of her father. She had quickly learned never to ask such an insulting question of this well-bred man.

"My dear young woman," he said. "If I did not judge that you had a fine talent, I would not be standing here wasting my valuable time by addressing you!"

Lindsay had meekly apologized.

By now all of Washington knew she was back in town—sans Alec Clarke. But Lindsay had found that she had matured and could greet a quick question or photograph from the press with a slight smile and brief reply and hurry on to her business. She was pleased with this accomplishment and no longer felt that the press was interfering with her life. She refused all dates, pleading too great an involvement with her work. But deep down she knew she would only look into another man's face and see sharply appraising pitch-black eyes laughing at her and a slightly mocking grin on a bronzed, angular face.

Susan Chatfield

Tonight was her opening and she was unusually calm, almost indifferent toward the outcome. She had asked Linton to sell all the paintings he could. She wanted no reminders of this fall in her life. She had only kept one of her pencil sketches—the one of Jason—and that was framed and hidden in her closet. She couldn't bear the thought of someone else having it. She would send it to Jake as a Christmas present.

For the opening she had chosen this gown of pure silk. The mandarin collar stood high against her slim white neck, and the gown flowed softly against her body in simple lines to the floor. It covered her completely yet revealed her curves like a second silky skin of turquoise to match her eyes. The shell sleeves emphasized the translucent whiteness of her slim arms. She wore no jewelry except for pearls dangling from a bamboo stick placed in her black hair, which she wore high on her head in keeping with the Chinese style of her dress.

Gazing at her face, she made sure the slight bluish circles under her eyes had been skillfully covered with pale makeup. She had added a pale turquoise eyeshadow and black mascara to accent her eyes, hoping to take away the obvious paleness in her face. A peach blusher on her cheekbones had helped somewhat, and the final touch of a clear coral lip gloss had completed the look she wanted.

A hand rapped on her door, and she turned to greet her father. He cleared his throat and walked over to her, his arms extended.

"No need to tell you, my dear, how proud of you I am. I only wish your mother could be here now to enjoy this evening with us. You look beautiful. Very regal, you know. What smells so good?"

Lindsay smiled and reached down to show him the bottle of Fidji that he had bought for her. She raised her eyebrows and a grin of mischief lit her face.

"You have good taste, Father. I had to wear it tonight of all nights. For luck!" She walked into her father's arms and he gave her a bear hug. He cleared his throat and stepped back.

176

"Well, everyone who is anyone will be there by now. No use putting it off. Shall we go, my dear?"

Nodding, Lindsay reached over and drew on her matching quilted evening coat and they walked down the stairs arm in arm.

Emerson opened the door with a slight bow and said coolly, "Good luck, Miss Lindsay. We'll all be thinking of you!" She smiled her thanks and they hurried in the crisp December air toward the limousine.

Washington was a city of lights as they moved through it, a city of parties and pre-holiday festivities. As they pulled up to the gallery, Lindsay saw that most of the persons invited had arrived. Many formally dressed people could be seen milling around and talking through the well-lit, long gallery windows. They quickly walked inside and Harold Linton greeted them.

The gallery was a two-story room, very airy and spacious. Crystal chandeliers hung suspended from the ceiling and accented the brilliance of the many paintings placed around the walls. Lindsay circulated among the guests, looking for familiar faces and smiling to everyone who had come. Champagne flowed freely and so did the conversation. After an hour or so, Lindsay felt as if her smile had frozen permanently on her face, and that the din would soon deafen her. As she passed people standing before her paintings, she heard soft words of praise and appreciation. She wondered how much longer the party would go on and recalled that Mr. Linton had warned her that it would be improper of her to leave before the last guest did. Glancing around at the large silver trays of hors d'oeuvres and the tall glasses of champagne being served to the guests, she knew the evening would be a long one. She was still circulating and joining small groups to discuss her paintings when she heard Mr. Linton call for everyone's attention.

"Please everyone, your attention, if you please? Thank you. It is my great privilege to announce that we have a very special guest tonight, one whose work is well known in the art world. He has taken a very special interest in the work of Miss Sheffield and I also happen to know that she had no idea he would be here tonight."

Lindsay's heart seemed to stop and she found herself holding her breath painfully as she stared at Linton. It couldn't be, she thought, hoping wildly. Her eyes widened as she glanced behind Linton, who stepped aside to allow her father and another man walk into the room.

"Ladies and gentlemen, Mr. Jake Mainwaring of Vermont."

Lindsay took in the sheepish grin on the freckled face and the thatch of reddish hair on the short man, dressed formally in a black tuxedo. She rushed over to him, her face animated with delight.

"Uncle Jake, you devil. I thought you were in Greece. How on earth did you find out about tonight? Oh, I'm so glad to see you." Words became difficult as she felt tears brim, close to falling, and she stepped back from his arms, finding herself unconsciously glancing over and around his shoulders for another face. She returned her eyes to his own shrewd ones, and they sparkled back at her with deep brown lights.

"Why, Lindsay, honey, who else are you looking for? I thought I'd be enough of a surprise for you!" His soft brown eyes took in her pale face.

"Oh, you are, darling. I'm so glad to see you! Why didn't you let me know you were coming?" She glanced at her father suddenly, noting the benign look on his face. "Father! You knew all about this. You told Jake about tonight!"

He smiled and beamed down on his daughter, enjoying her pleasure. "Of course I did. I like to surprise you, especially when I know you're going to be pleasantly surprised."

"I understand you met Jason when you came up to the cabin, my dear. Smartest thing you ever did, you know—that is deciding to paint, not meeting Jason. He's getting married, you know, although I can't really understand why. He's always been such a loner." Jake's voice trickled off as his sharp eyes wandered around the room, flicking from one painting to the other, typically unaware of what the conversation was about as his interest was quickly taken by the one thing he loved more than anything in the world—art.

Lindsay forced a trembling smile to her lips, and tried to shake off the effect of his unthinking words about Jason. "Father, why don't you take Uncle Jake around? I can see he's anxious to comment on the value of my work."

Her father nodded and frowned suddenly at her. "You seem a bit wan, my dear. Why don't you take a breather upstairs in Linton's study? I'll represent the family for a while."

She nodded gratefully and turned toward the long staircase. She heard her name being called and halted for a moment as she saw a familiar person walking toward her with quick strides. Her eyes widened quickly and she opened her mouth to say, "Alec! I didn't know you were here. When did you arrive? I haven't seen you milling around."

He stood over her, his cool blue eyes gazing down at her. As they were bumped by the crowd, he took hold of her elbow and walked her to the staircase.

"Lindsay, we have to talk, please," he said. "If only for a moment. I have something to say to you. Is there somewhere private where we can talk?" His anxious eyes beseeched her and she nodded wearily.

"All right, Alec, but we really have nothing to discuss. I was just going upstairs to the study to rest for a while. This din is giving me a headache." She preceded him, wondering why he had shown up tonight. As far as she was concerned, the past was over—all of it. She entered the dimly lit study and looked at the fireplace across the room. It was lit and two tall, comfortable chairs were facing it, the backs to her. She decided not to sit down, knowing that Alec would take advantage of the situation and stay too long. She wanted to be alone. She turned to him and said quietly, "Now, what is it, Alec? I understand from my father that you've been doing quite well in your new position. I'm glad for you. You've a brilliant mind and will go far in politics." She smiled slightly, amazed at how easily this conversation was going. She felt completely in control while Alec seemed ill at ease.

He reached out and took her slim hand in his, stepping closer to her. His long finger reached out and traced her cheekbone. "You've lost weight, but you're still as beautiful as ever. Your father told me you had been ill, but he would never tell me where you were after you left. Oh, Lindsay, it's been hell without you. You left and wouldn't let me explain anything."

She interrupted softly. "There was nothing to explain, Alec. I think everything was fairly self-explanatory, don't you?"

His eyes dropped and he shook his head. "I know how it looked, and I was wrong not to tell you about my gambling debts, but Lindsay, my darling, I loved you so much and I wanted you to think the world of me. I just couldn't tell you the truth. I haven't gambled since and I'll always be eternally grateful to your father for giving me a second chance. But I need to know, Lindsay darling. Will you give me a second chance?"

She looked at him, feeling nothing but pity. Gone was the hurt and the anger. Love for another, much stronger man had wiped it from her mind and heart. She shook her head slightly and gently removed her hand from his.

"Please, Lindsay, say you'll forgive me. I need you so much!"

An icy, very familiar voice pierced the quiet of the room. It came from someone sitting in the high-backed chairs in front of the roaring fire!

"Consider yourself forgiven, Mr. Clarke. Now get out of here."

Lindsay froze, unable to turn around. Her heart skipped wildly and her lips quivered as blood pounded in her head. She closed her eyes, knowing that voice with all its moods and loving it, even when it was directed at her in anger.

Her breath became ragged as she heard Alec murmur in anger, "Who the hell do you think you are, intruding in on

180

a private conversation? And how do you know who I am?" Alec peered into the darkness toward the tall figure who was softly treading across the room to stop just behind Lindsay. She thought she would faint at Jason's nearness, yet still she could neither speak nor move.

She heard Jason's quietly menacing voice take on a softly dangerous note. "If Miss Sheffield wants me to leave, she can always ask me to. Tell me, Lindsay, do you want me to leave or would you prefer Mr. Clarke to go?"

She could feel the dark intensity of his gaze burning through her and she whispered softly, "Please, Alec, there's nothing more to say. Please go."

Alec's face turned white with fury as he glared first at Lindsay and then at the fiercely dark man standing firmly behind her. Muttering a sharp expletive, Alec turned and marched out of the room.

Strong fingers rested lightly on Lindsay's shoulders and turned her around. She opened her eyes and they rested on Jason's darkly handsome face. His eyes took in her pale beauty and then ran lightly and quickly over her slender body.

"You *have* lost weight, and you *are* still as beautiful as ever. I missed you, kitten." So casually said, yet her heart was breaking into little pieces again. She forced herself away from him and walked over to the fire. He followed.

"What are you doing here, Jason?" she asked. "This is even more of a surprise than Jake's appearing. I understand from him that you're getting married soon. Is Marcia with you?" She forced herself to stand away from him, aware of how devastating his lightest touch could be. She looked into his dark eyes and saw the firelight and something else flashing in them.

He cocked his head to one side and thrust his lean hands into the pockets of his suit. He looked as if he was born to wear a black tuxedo, with his dark, angular face and throat bordered by the stark whiteness of his shirt. She knew how much he hated to wear clothes like this. Her heart caught in her throat as he studied her and finally, after pursing his firm lips together, smiled and walked over to stand directly in front of her. There was nowhere for her to turn. The fire was to her back and Jason blocked every means of escape. She felt his hard hands reach out and take her by the waist. She found her eyes glued to his chest. Her chin started to tremble, and her legs felt weak at his touch. Jason whispered softly, his lips held against the softness of her cheek, moving toward her ear, leaving a trail of fire in their wake. She found her hands reaching up to grasp the lapels of his jacket for support. Did he have any idea what he was doing to her?

"No, I have no idea what Marcia is doing at the moment. I am here because I planned on being with you the night you had your first show. It's been hell, waiting these past weeks for all of this to come about. Many times I almost took off and came down here, but your father dissuaded me. He said I would ruin everything."

Lindsay listened, confused by his words. "My father? But my father hasn't mentioned you since I came back. You mean you would have come down here to see me but my *father* kept you away?"

Jason chuckled softly, stopping for a moment to explore the shell of her ear with his lips. Lindsay felt herself melt and moved closer to Jason. It was no good. She couldn't fight the sensations he was awakening in her.

"Yes, it was Ray's idea to allow you the time to get your show completed. He said if I came down before then I would take your mind off your work and spoil everything. It was my idea in the first place for you to come home and 'find yourself' and he was right, but then, he was being entirely objective about it and I was too subjective—too emotionally involved, I guess. But I swore I would be here tonight, and I am. Are you happy with how everything is working out tonight, Lindsay? Do you really believe you have a career in art as you had hoped?"

Lindsay found that she could only whisper. "Yes. It seems to be going well; at least, Mr. Linton says people are interested in buying some of my paintings. It was kind of you to take an interest in the outcome, Jason. It was quite a trip to make just to see if I could sell a few paintings."

"Oh, it was worth it. I had a great deal invested in this trip, you see. You've sold more than a few paintings. Linton tells me that most of them have been sold."

Confused, she drew back her head and looked up into his dancing eyes. "What do you mean, Linton told *you*? Why would he tell you about my paintings, Jason? He's notorious for never divulging any information about a painting he has sold, neither the price nor the buyer. Why is he suddenly reporting to you?"

Her eyes held a slightly accusing look in them and a grin came to his dark face as he answered casually, "Because, Lindsay my love, he was instructed by me to tell anyone who was interested in purchasing one of your works that it was already sold. Every one of your works that would have been bought by someone else tonight was topped by me. I bought every painting that would have left the collection. Now it will stay intact."

"But why, Jason? Why would you want to buy those paintings? What could they possibly mean to you? Oh, you're just interfering again, taking over, damn you." She tried to pull away from him, but he grabbed her wrist in a viselike grip and pulled her over to him and down onto his lap as he sat quickly into the chair by the fire.

"There you go again, jumping to conclusions, woman. Will you stop squirming and listen to me for once in your life? I want those paintings because they are the first ones you ever did, and they represent the fall that I fell in love with you. Yes, in love with you, damn it. Since the night I found you asleep on the sofa with the firelight flickering off that beautiful face of yours. You've been driving me insane since that night. You're obstinate and perplexing and infuriating and I love every inch of you. You exasperate the hell out of me and it's about all I can do to keep my hands off you. No, keep your mouth shut for one more moment or I'll kiss it shut and then I'll never get out what I've been waiting to say since October. I need you and I want you. I've certainly never said otherwise. But you weren't ready for any commitment, regardless of how you were attracted to me. I knew you had to come back here to the place and the things that you had run away from. You had to face them. Once you had done that, I knew I could ask you to come back to me."

Lindsay forced the words out of her dry mouth. "But what about Marcia? You love her and you're going to marry her. How can you sit here and tell me you love me? I heard you tell her in your house that day that you loved her. And you even told me that you intended to marry!"

Her lips were suddenly sealed with a hot, searing brand of possession by his hard lips. She felt her arms rise to wind themselves around his neck as she responded with all the pent-up emotions that she had kept under the surface for so many weeks. They could not get enough of each other, and she found her fingers unbuttoning his shirt to slide her fingers between the silky material to the hard muscles of his chest. His lips explored her neck as his fingers moved against her silk-covered breasts. She heard him exclaim softly, "Damn this dress," and he broke off, pulling back to catch the passion-glazed look in her eyes.

He shook his head to clear it and continued, whispering against the head that he held closely to his lips, caressing her hairline with his warm breath.

"I never told Marica that I loved her. I was just teaching you a lesson for eavesdropping again. I heard you tiptoe to the staircase and, if you'll remember correctly, I said I would do anything for the woman I loved, and that included teaching her a well-deserved lesson. The day after we slept together I did admit I had intended to marry, but I never told you to whom. Once again you just assumed it was Marcia and I decided it would be better if you could return home thinking there was no future for the two of us. That way you would devote yourself entirely to your art. And now I'm here and now I can ask you to marry me, and I'd better not be wrong about how you really feel about me."

"But how can you be so sure of how I really feel about

you, Jason? Perhaps this is just a sexual thing. And what about all those dinners and things with Marcia?"

A grin lit his face as he patiently explained, "I was building a house for close friends of Marcia's father. You heard her mention Edward and his wife. It was purely business, although I'll not deny that before you came up to Vermont there was more than a casual relationship between Marcia and myself. But I stopped seeing her after I realized that I was falling in love with an innocent who couldn't even sit in a canoe right! And yes, Jake did say that I was getting married, but then he knew *whom* I was planning on settling down with! And as for the final question—am I sure that you love me—yes, I am. There was one piece of art missing from the collection downstairs. I went over the whole kit and caboodle much earlier with Linton. There's a particular sketch—a penciled one—of a face that I look at every morning when I shave. I assume it's me—at least it sure as hell had better be me—and I remember something you told me—that you would never be able to truly draw or paint anything that you didn't really love. Was I right, kitten?"

His black eyes demanded her response and she raggedly took in a breath and nodded her dark head. "You seem to have everything figured out, don't you, Jason. I've loved you since that day we fell into the lake, and I had no idea that you felt the same way. But Jason, you and Dad were wrong. You should have told me before I came back to Washington. I've never been through such an awful time in my life, wanting you, trying not to think of you, thinking you loved someone else. It really wasn't fair."

His lips moved to just a fraction away from her own and he whispered softly and possessively, "Then, I'll just have to make up for that lost time, won't I?" His lips burned against her own with fiery passion as he settled her more closely on his lap.

A few moments later, Lindsay thought she heard her father's voice coming from outside the door, passing on down the hallway. Her ears were burning from the expertise of Jason's lovemaking, and the sound of her father's voice made a whirling noise as she settled down against his hard body, reaching for his head to draw it to her again.

Faintly the disappearing words could be heard. "Well, Jake, I think there's a bottle of very old brandy in one of these rooms. I think we both have a great deal to celebrate by now, don't you?"

She heard her uncle's answering chuckle and sighed.

LOOK FOR NEXT MONTH'S
CANDLELIGHT ECSTASY ROMANCES™:

Candlelight Ecstasy Romances

Love—the way you want it!

Candlelight Romances